Thousands of Tears

A True Story of International Abduction and Miraculous Rescue

Maria T. Nicholas

authorHOUSE™

1663 LIBERTY DRIVE, SUITE 200
BLOOMINGTON, INDIANA 47403
(800) 839-8640
WWW.AUTHORHOUSE.COM

First published by AuthorHouse 07/08/05

ISBN: 1-4208-3982-9 (sc)

Library of Congress Control Number: 2005902318

Printed in the United States of America
Bloomington, Indiana

This book is printed on acid-free paper.

CONTENTS

WITH GRATITUDE

I trust that these pages will be a source of inspiration to you. This true life story has touched the lives of thousands of people. It's the kind of story that never gets old, and as people hear it over and over again, the tears begin to appear; a true sign of a heart-felt moment.

This book is the result of a conviction I have had for some years now to write but couldn't get started. I felt like I was hiding this incredible miracle that many other people needed to hear and be encouraged by. Yet, the stress of life and the lack of motivation and time held me back.

Due to a series of events that occurred, the thought of writing this book became even dimmer. Yet I knew I needed to write it. With perseverance and determination the breakthrough finally came.

I am eternally grateful for the privilege of knowing Corine and Nelson Jackson whose persistent prayers, support and friendship during those hard times without Anna will never be forgotton. Corine's encouragement to me that I would write this book, before she passed into eternity, is one of the main reasons it has now been completed. Her absence from this earth has left a void that can never be replaced. She was like my guardian angel who watched over me so faithfully with persistent, fervent prayers that were answered. My sincere, deep gratitude for her can only be expressed when I see her one day in heaven.

I owe an immense debt of gratitude to Mark Miller from the American Association for Lost Children. I would not have had a story to write without his help. His dedication and love for missing children is something I will always value and hold dear. He holds a special place in our hearts. I will always be grateful for his generous, considerate, and caring ways. His selflessness and love for the Lord are also very admirable traits. It is impossible to say enough thanks to him. I will never forget how he risked his life to go in search of Anna. He will always be "Uncle Mark" to us. Words are inadequate to express our heartfelt gratitude to him. "Mark, there is a special award awaiting you in heaven."

Words cannot suffice to express my deep gratitude to Susan Cohen, the attorney who helped me gain custody of AnnaMaria. Her compassion and concern for women in distress as I was, speak volumes. Thanks for the passion you expressed in the process of the law in trying to see Anna restored to me.

A heart-felt thanks to Detective Lupo, for simply following through with details in our case in such a conscientious way. Thanks for helping to dispel many of the apprehensions I had in the legal system.

This story might not have been written without the help of George and Mary Donovan. I especially want to thank them for their generosity in affording me the time to write this book. They are two of the most wonderful, generous people I have ever met. Their kindness is beyond description. Words can never fully express our love and appreciation for all the things they have done for us. My only hope is that the Lord will repay them someday.

To Lily, my right arm, who has been there for us so many times through all the ups and downs that we faced. I now know what true friendship really means. I will always remember her loyal, helpful, and caring ways, especially during those difficult moments of the trial. I will never forget how she watched over Anna and David. We could not have survived some of the storms we faced without her. Anna and David will always cherish those playful times of pillow fights they had with her. They are convinced that no one can outdo Auntie Lily's tickles. I hope we will still be able to have our special cup of tea together even when we are old. There are not enough thanks in this world to give her. She will always have an extra special place in our hearts.

I want to thank my brother, Nick, for all his help over the years. Thanks for all the laughs and free medical advice over the phone. I also want to thank my mother for all her help, good cooking and encouragement over the years. Thanks to Kay, my sister, for babysitting at times and Nicky for keeping us laughing. I want to especially thank Golda and Mariano for being there when we needed to be rescued.

Many thanks to my friends, Ernie and Judy, Carol and Rusty, Kregg an Tesse, Gary and Joanne, Don and Betty, Val, Claudette, Ann, Diana, Mary, Hannele and Angela who have all encouraged me for a long time to write this book. In fact, Judy would say to me at times, "This story should be a movie." Thanks to Georgia for providing a hiding place for us in Jamaica and to Bishop Herro Blair for all his prayers.

I also want to thank Russ and Carol Shinpoch for believing in this story and wanting the women at Wildwood to hear it. I was truly encouraged by all their responses to write this book.

I especially want to thank Tony Stinson, my Pastor, for his wise counsel to me regarding getting my manuscript published. I appreciate so much the time he took from his extremely busy schedule to answer my emails and review the agreement before I signed it. Your gracious attitude will always be remembered.

A heart-felt thanks to my friends, Kyla and Robin Nelson, for the wonderful job they did on the article about this story for *Conversations* magazine. It will surely prove to be a useful marketing tool for the book. I especially want to thank Robin for his creative insight and talents in helping to design the cover of the book. I remember his words to me so well, "I want to design the cover of your book." Thanks for the encouragement that "it will happen." Our favorite part in that whole process was the photo shoots; we were made to feel like celebrities.

I am especially grateful to Ryan Noffsinger, who did an outstanding job in the graphic design for the cover of the book. I appreciate so much all the time he devoted in helping me work out the final details in order to get this book in production amidst his busy schedule.

I want to thank all the ladies, especially Dana, in my Women of Grace fusion group at Wildwood Baptist church who prayed so faithfully for this book to be published. To Angela who always wanted to know if I was in the closet writing; I finally got it done. I won't ever forget those special prayer walks with Cindy and Carol. Thanks to Shirley for taking the time to preview the manuscript and expressing that it was a tear jerker. I appreciate so much Carlene's effort in arranging speaking engagements and wanting everyone to hear this story.

I appreciate so much the help I received from Andy Ledford who made copies of a video clip about Anna's return from Germany. They served as important marketing tools.

I want to thank AuthorHouse for making it possible for first-time authors like me to get my voice in print. Special thanks to Leslie Bolton, for the painstaking job of cleaning up my manuscript. A special thank you to: Kyle Snyder, Robert Edwards, Clark Clarkson and Kris Geist for all their help and timely responses to all my questions. I also want to thank Becky Lehr for putting on the special finishing touches. Thanks for alleviating all my fears and apprehensions about the publishing process. It has truly been a pleasure working with all of you.

Most of all, I want to thank my three wonderful children, Malaika, AnnaMaria, and David for all their support and encouragement over the years. They have always believed in me when I was losing confidence in myself. They were the winds beneath my wings. Thanks for all the encouraging cards of appreciation, guys. I hold a special thank you to David for all the much needed "energy" hugs and prayers when I thought I was fading. He is truly a son of consolation. Many, many, special thanks to Anna for all her thoughtful, helpful ways and special touches that can never be duplicated. I thank the Lord each day for the miracle that she is. An abundance of thanks to Malaika for her encouragement over the years and for helping me to regain confidence when I thought it was lost. All the suggestions and painstaking editing she did on the manuscript are so much appreciated. Her contributions have been invaluable. Her name Malaika, which means "angel," was so appropriately given. She has truly been one to me at times.

Words are inadequate to describe my deep gratitude to God, who being all powerful, orchestrated these incredible events. I am constantly overcome by sheer wonder of His power and magnificence.

* * *

I will be grateful to Him forever for what He has done for me.

PREFACE

This is a true story about my daughter, AnnaMaria, who was secretly taken, without my permission, to another country by her father for five years and three months.

Whenever I tell this story, whether to an individual or a large or small group of people, the reactions have always been the same: "You need to write a book." Those words have been stuck in my mind for ten years now, and I finally realized that this remarkable story must be heard, and I needed to write it.

It offers hope for difficult circumstances as hard and as painful as this was for me, her mother. It will renew one's confidence to start trusting again and will confirm that there is a God who keeps His promises and yes, answers prayers.

This is a modern-day miracle. You will see how, after turning to eleven organizations for assistance, my help finally came from the Lord. You will be encouraged not to lose faith if your circumstances seem impossible or so dark that you feel there is no hope.

I had come to the end of my rope after receiving bad news that the FBI was no longer interested in my case. I felt like giving up because all doors were closed, and I thought I'd never see my child again. It was when I became helpless that God proved Himself mighty.

I'm forever grateful for His unfailing love and faithfulness in restoring AnnaMaria to me. It is His doing, and it is His story. He orchestrated all the events for me to get her back. I will praise Him forever for what He has done. All glory and honor are due unto His Name.

In the past few months, I felt that I should start writing parts of this story as they occurred. At first, it seemed like an insurmountable task, but as I began, the Lord gave me the grace to continue, and His presence was felt even in the hard-to-bear parts of it.

My hope is that this story will touch you, and that before you get to the last page, you will know that if God could perform such a miracle for me, He can do the same for you.

Maria Nicholas
Atlanta, November 2003

I dedicate this book to my three wonderful children: Malaika, AnnaMaria, and David who are special gifts to me from the Lord. They have been my greatest supporters and encouragers throughout these difficult years

"Oh Lord," I cried, "if you created the heavens, the earth, the animals, and man in relation to all that, then this is not too difficult for you to do. I will not give up until you bring Anna back."

December 9, 2004

MOM,

You mean the world to me.
When I feel like I can't go on,
I remember all you went through for me.
You are my hero.
I hope you have the best birthday ever!

I love you so much.
Thanks for being my mom.

♥ Anna

CHAPTER 1

MIDNIGHT THREAT AND ESCAPES

It was a long and stressful day of wondering where Paul could be with AnnaMaria since I had not heard from him in 24 hours. I was lying on the sofa at my niece's apartment with a myriad of thoughts going through my head. One of those thoughts centered on him absconding with her to Jamaica. I couldn't bear to think about it. I was so restless that I could hardly sleep.

It was about twenty minutes past midnight when the phone finally rang. My niece, Golda, answered it and informed me it was for me. I could feel my heart pounding as I picked up the phone with the greatest apprehension.

"Hello?"

The voice at the other end of the phone had a distinctly sinister tone. "Maria, this is Paul," my estranged husband said. "I have AnnaMaria with me in Kingston, and she will never return to the United States. If you try anything, I will kill you!"

"Paul, what is wrong with you? Why are you speaking like this? You have violated my trust! You have Anna in Jamaica?" I gasped in shock, not wanting to believe what I had just heard. He repeated his threat as I felt myself seething with rage. He had secretly flown with our daughter to his homeland in the Caribbean to stay with his family.

My voice trembled as I asked to speak with his mother since each plea on my part was thwarted with another threat. I wanted to maintain my composure so I opted to communicate with her.

"Maria, I'm not a party to this," his mother quickly responded. "I was out at a tea party, my dear, and when I arrived home, I saw Paul on the verandah with AnnaMaria." She assured me Anna was fine but promised to question her son about his bizarre actions. "Don't worry yourself, dear, it will all work out." She said goodbye, and I heard the click of the phone, but I was motionless. I felt very desperate and helpless. I knew the nightmare had begun. It would be more than five years before I would see my precious child again.

ENOUGH WAS ENOUGH

It had been a long time coming; I could no longer stay in the marriage. My former husband had made it a way of life to intimidate me with arrogance, to plague me with mental abuse, and worst of all, to cause me to be suspicious of his behavior. I was seven months pregnant with our second child and AnnaMaria was barely ten months old when I decided to separate from him. Once I had made the decision to leave him, it was several weeks before Anna and I could make our escape.

My niece, Golda, and I had grown to be close friends in the recent years of living in neighboring communities in South Florida. She listened to my cry for several months. She was aware of my growing desperation in the marriage and that I could no longer tolerate the repeated intimidations. She recalled one night when he interrogated me for over three hours regarding his application for United States citizenship. I was planning to withdraw the sponsorship I had filed for him as his American wife. Somehow, he found out about it and became outraged. The interrogation and threats went on for what seemed like an eternity. He was physically so threatening that night, I truly thought he would resort to hitting me. Thank God he finally went to sleep.

3

I deserved better than that. I needed a kind, caring husband, not a character-disordered personality. I needed someone I could communicate with instead of feeling as if I were the maid. I wanted out. My sanity was more important to me at this point; I needed some peace of mind. I had such awful remorse about marrying him. These feelings were becoming too much to bear.

What was I thinking of when I decided to marry him spontaneously? My niece, who was engaged and vacationing in Jamaica, wanted to have a double ceremony there in Jamaica before returning to New York. I must have lost my mind temporarily. How did I circumvent my suspicions about him?

I had heard stories about his treatment of other women. I didn't heed any of them. I even had a dream before we were married that *he was seeing another woman* and in the dream *he was my husband*. I told him about it, and he laughed and said, "If you ever marry me I would never look at another woman."

I have never encountered this form of "honesty" and "sincerity," the kind in which a man tells a woman whatever it takes, just to get the desired response: "Yes."

AN ANGEL FORCED TO FLIGHT

My older daughter, Malaika, from a previous marriage, had overheard all that went on the night Paul had intimidated me. She later told me that she was trying to tape the conversation but couldn't from where she was in her bedroom. She was assumed to be asleep throughout the entire tirade that took place that night. Instead, she heard the threats he made, and she was determined at that moment that she would not be around to find out if they were real. She was afraid to disclose her plan to me, because she knew I would never allow her to leave by herself. After all, she was only fourteen years old.

I went into her room to sleep on the spare bed, as I could not bear to be in the same room with him after his display that night. Ironically, I was also lying there, scheming in my own mind an escape plot for all of us to get out of the horrible situation together. I, too, could not risk telling Malaika of this plan. The stakes were too high, and I feared she may tout something to Paul in all her frustrations and reveal our plans to him. That was the last thing I needed now, Paul watching my every move.

Later on the following morning, she was nagging me for her letters which Paul had confiscated for over two months.

The letters amounted to nothing more than silly teenage talk about who liked which boy. We got into an argument over these letters because I was reluctant to return them to her even though I had found where he had them hidden on top of the credenza in the living room. In retrospect, I was scared of repercussions from him. She was now annoyed with me, and since she had planned to leave, there was no chance of her talking to me about it at that point. The timing just could not have been worse.

She realized Paul did not want her around. He made it quite clear to her at times. As loving and as cooperative as she was, he always found fault with her. She could never please him. She was obedient and restrained herself from being disrespectful to him because of the way I trained her.

His ideal family was never to include her but should consist only of him, Anna, and me. When Malaika tried to entertain Anna at times in her swing, he would chase her away, saying, "Leave her alone."

At only fourteen years old, he wanted to put her in a boarding school to get rid of her. He became intensely jealous of my relationship with her, my first born child, who was the closest person to me during the years before I met Paul. I struggled to keep her close to me, but he always found a way to exclude her. Needless to say, she suffered much rejection emotionally. At one point, I had to remove her from the house on his command, or else he would have physically hurt her.

A few minutes after Malaika and I had had our little tussle, she went into her bathroom and started taking a shower. I came into her bathroom momentarily, having no idea what was about to transpire. She said nothing. I said nothing. My mind was scanning several things all at once. I was still recovering from Paul's tyranny the night before, while attempting to quiet my teenager's frustrations, feed my ten month-old who was discovering the art of walking, and survive my third trimester of pregnancy. Little did I know that AnnaMaria had already received a hundred goodbye kisses.

When breakfast was ready, I knocked on her bedroom door which was locked but there was no answer. I knocked a few more times, and there was still no answer, so I decided to walk around the side of the house and peek through her bedroom window to see what she was doing. I called out her name a few times, and there was still no answer. Then I saw the window ajar and realized she was gone. My heart started pounding fast as I ran back into the house to get the keys for Paul's truck to try and go after her. The keys were no where to be found so I decided to knock on the door where Paul was sleeping, and he eventually opened it. I asked him to let me have his keys, and he wanted to know why, so I told him I believed Malaika left the house.

His response was, "Let her go. I'm not going to give you the keys to go after her."

I was seven months pregnant and had difficulty walking because of a strained muscle in my left leg. I felt so helpless that I couldn't go and try to find her. I just sat and cried.

I eventually went into her bedroom after Paul unlocked the door, feeling desperate, not knowing what to do, and found this note she had left for me on her bed. It read:

> *Dear Mom,*
>
> *I'm sorry for asking stupid questions this morning. Tell Uncle Paul to cherish those letters to his heart if he wants to because I don't need them. The same way you don't need me to bother you. And since that's the case, I'll leave you alone in peace. Good luck in everything, don't worry about me, I'll find someone who wants a stupid 14 year old, ok? ☺ Maybe it just didn't work out. No hard feelings, ok. I really ♥ you, but I don't feel any ♥ coming back, so see you in a few years.*
>
> *♥ ya lots,*
> *Malaika*

She finally made it over to a shopping center close to the house. She then called my niece but only heard the voicemail greeting. My daughter had the same plan as me initially! When she found that no one was home, she made a collect call to my brother, Nick, who lived in Michigan. She told him what had happened and also how Paul had been treating her. He, being an established surgeon, had the means by which to get her to Michigan, He immediately called a friend who was living in Hollywood, Florida, and had her purchase a ticket for her.

So on June 29th,1986, at around 12:00 noon, Malaika left the house and later on that day boarded a plane and was headed to Kalamazoo, Michigan. She stayed with my brother for a few days, and he wouldn't let me speak with her for fear I would pressure her to return.

He thought the circumstances under which she was living were unhealthy so he decided to take things into his own hands. He kept making excuses that she was out with friends and that he would have her give me a call. In the meantime, he was making arrangements to have her sent to her father who lived in Kingston, Jamaica. Of course, I was not happy with that idea and was very upset with him for some time.

She finally called from Michigan about three days later. Paul was on one extension threatening to turn Malaika over to the police, telling her she would wind up in juvenile hall.

I was on the other extension, screaming desperately into the phone, "Malaika, you get back on that plane and come home immediately!"

Malaika's only reply was, "Sorry, Mom, I can't come back right now. I need to be away from that man for a long time." Malaika could only hear Paul's threats, again and again over the telephone. I knew she would not return with him around me. Instead, she agreed for her uncle Nick to send her to live with her father in Jamaica.

SUSPICIONS

One morning, about four days later, while I was in the kitchen, I overheard Paul speaking softly with someone on the phone from the bedroom. Curiosity got the better of me so I carefully picked up the phone in the kitchen, so as not to be discovered in an attempt to eavesdrop. I needed to know who he was speaking with in order to confirm my suspicions. I heard a female voice asking him what time he would be getting there and what was taking him so long. His response was that he would be leaving shortly.

I wanted to intercept and ask her a few questions and perhaps scream a bit in her ears, but instead, I quietly put the phone back on the receiver and continued preparing Anna's food. There is no way I could fully explain what I felt hearing another woman's voice on the phone. It was not a voice I recognized, so who could it be? Was this some secret person he was hiding from me and hoping I wouldn't find out about? That tone painted a rather suspicious picture in my mind especially when I heard the questions she asked him. I was speechless and felt incapable of responding. I was devastated and was beginning to experience the initial stages of anger. It was as if someone had taken my heart and squeezed it into a tiny ball. It felt frozen. Whatever was left of it resounded with loud thumps in my chest. I felt so hurt, wounded, and betrayed. I was devastated.

I was immediately reminded of the unborn child I was carrying. His sudden rapid and intense movements I felt inside of me were indications that he was also experiencing distress. I took a deep breath for his sake and forced myself to stay calm. I had no choice but to try and think about his welfare, also, in my helpless and severely distressed state. How sad that I was experiencing such emotional discomfort being seven months pregnant. I should have been happy and enjoying my pregnancy. Instead, I was depressed and constantly crying. I felt as if I were carrying a huge burden weighing thousands of pounds that I couldn't wait to put down.

I regained some temporary composure, and it occurred to me that wisdom should take its course. After all, one who knows better should do better. What would I have achieved besides denial if I confronted him? Why should I have put myself through what could have been described as a regrettable moment? After all, I had experienced his past outbursts. I knew how traumatizing they were. I would be the one to suffer more, being pregnant. The conversation I overheard on the telephone only confirmed my suspicions of extra-marital behavior.

Deceitfulness is so destructive and knows no boundaries. I suppose he was just behaving like some of his counterparts back home in Jamaica. The typical scenario tolerated by our society there was that of the arrogant patriarch who ill-treated his devoted wife while he romanced his mistress(es). It appeared as if he had learned from them, for sure. No woman, as he once said to me, would ever tell him what to do. In effect, he felt he had a license to destroy a marriage and the lives involved. He had no regard for the process of communication. How many times before had I suggested that we go for counseling, but he refused to cooperate? His presumptuous response once was that he could teach the counselor a few things and that he didn't need one.

He came into the kitchen moments later and told me he would be gone for most of the day. He did not say where he was going or what he was going to do, and so as to avoid an argument with him, I asked no questions. I did not show any negative emotions in an effort not to put him on guard, but simply nodded my head, as if to say okay. I had a plan, and my mind was made up. We would have to wait for the perfect opportunity to leave. The timing now would be crucial.

I spent the day as efficiently as possible, packing some of my personal things and keeping them in their original places. I organized my clothes and had them ready to be thrown in bags at the appointed time. My suits and dresses were grouped together with ties that could be easily removed from the closet in a hurry. I also prepared AnnaMaria's belongings. I asked my niece's husband, Mariano, to bring a screwdriver in order to dismantle her crib. I also hid an extra copy of her birth certificate in the linen closet, for fear he would seize it, which I planned to remove on my departure. He had taken the original one from me. I was much smarter than he was, I thought. If he had a plan, I had already formulated a counter-plan. Little did I know that I was about to make a costly miscalculation.

I discussed with my niece that they should arrange to come and get us after Paul had left for work at around 1:30 a.m. We agreed on the day and time but I was feeling a bit nervous about it so I called her after Paul left and told her I didn't feel comfortable leaving that day. I also mentioned to her that he had been rather combative and unreasonable the past few days, and he might just come back out of guilt to check and see if we were still there.

A few minutes after I finished speaking with Golda, I was lying in our bedroom when I heard him open the front door. I pretended to be asleep, and he came straight to the room where I was and opened the door. He saw that I was there, so he closed it back, went out through the front door, and took off in his truck again. I breathed a sigh of relief.

I immediately redialed Golda's number and told her what had happened, and we both realized that we would have been caught had we attempted to carry out our plans that night. Who knows what the consequences would have been? He might have hurt us in the process, given his temper. Besides, he would have taken Anna forcefully from me; it would surely have been a fiasco. I believe God spared us the unknown.

We decided to make our move two days later instead. It was July 16th,1986, and we were ready. Paul left for work and AnnaMaria was fast asleep. It was now about 1:15 a.m., and I was extremely nervous and felt a bit of trembling. I called Golda and told her it was time to go. She assured me that they were on their way; an estimated seven-minute drive. I went into the bathroom and prayed and asked the Lord to help us so that we would not get caught. I was riddled with fear and extremely nervous.

Golda and Mariano arrived, and we started working as quickly as we could. We took Anna out of her crib, and Mariano pulled it apart in a few minutes. Golda and I loaded the car with a few items.

After about 10 minutes, I said to Mariano, "Let me get my clothes in the back bedroom."

And he said, "No! We have no time for that. Let's get out of here! If Paul comes and finds us, we are dead."

The urgency in his voice was compelling. I was concerned as to what actions Paul might take; I, therefore, feared for my life. We were not about to take a chance so I followed his warning and that was the last I ever saw of my clothes. The risk was not worth it. After all, the most important thing at this moment was to get out of there with Anna. Clothes, I thought, could always be replaced.

We crammed all we could in their small Honda Civic and drove out of the subdivision. We kept looking all around us, even though it was dark, to see if Paul was watching us. We were all so nervous and finally breathed a sigh of relief once we turned on the main road to their apartment. At last, we were out of danger.

We finally arrived at the apartment and left everything in the car overnight. We stayed indoors until the next day.

Later on that morning, when Paul discovered that we were gone, he went over to my sister, Antonia's, house in Hollywood and started screaming hysterically wanting to know where we were. I deliberately excluded her from the escape plans for fear he would intimidate her to reveal our location. She started making phone calls trying to locate us but was unsuccessful right before his eyes. I spoke with her two days later, but I was not ready to reveal my safe hiding place. I specifically didn't tell any friends where we were staying because I knew Paul would force them to talk and then come looking for us. I feared for our safety.

Malaika eventually called me at the house where I was staying after arriving in Jamaica and told me she was with her dad. I told her I wanted her to come back to me because I was no longer at the house, but she thought perhaps I would return to Paul at some later date. She didn't trust the situation since I had returned once before after I had moved out with both her and Anna for about a month.

I asked to speak with her father. I made the same request to have her sent back to me, but he refused. He then pleaded with me to let her stay with him and finish high school in Jamaica. I told him as soon as I had the baby I would be on the next plane to Kingston to get her. He pleaded further to let him help me with Malaika at this stage since I had my hands full. I partially agreed, but I was not happy with the decision.

I received a message from Paul after several days in hiding indicating that he wanted to speak with me. I did not return his call because I was a bit apprehensive. I didn't want to hear his voice reprimanding or threatening me. I also knew he would upset me so I wanted to avoid speaking with him at all cost. I rehearsed his fits of temper in my mind and that made me more determined not to return his call. A few days later, his mother arrived from Jamaica and also called and left a message for me saying she would like to speak with me.

I returned her call, and during the course of our conversation, she asked me if she could see AnnaMaria. I agreed, on the condition that Anna would be left in her care, and that she would return her to me. She promised she would abide by my wishes.

I felt that I could trust his mother and that she would not tolerate any unprincipled behavior on his part, such as not returning AnnaMaria to me. His mother and I always got along well and, as I assumed, she was true to her word.

I brought Anna back to the house from where we had escaped so her grandmother could see her. It was a very strange feeling going back there, since I thought I would never see it again. My mind was instantly thrown into a flashback of those crucial ten minutes that we seized in order to make our exit. As I walked into the house, the feelings of apprehension and burden were weighing heavily, as if I had never left. I could not bear to look at Paul initially but tried to focus on his mother.

Paul, his sister, and his mother were in the living room when we arrived. The meeting was cordial, considering this was our first encounter with Paul since our *escape*. His mother asked if Anna could spend the night. I agreed and left shortly afterwards.

While I was driving out of the subdivision, I couldn't help the bizarre feelings I was having concerning Anna. I was wondering if they might take off with her. Then I thought, oh no, his mother wouldn't agree to anything like that. Then again, my mind rambled even more—what if Paul refused to give her back to me when I went to pick her up. I was a bit uncomfortable, to say the least. At this point, I could only hope for the best and pray everything would go well.

THE WILD MAN SHOWS HIS COLORS

When I went back to get Anna, she was sleeping. However, after a brief conversation with his mother and sister, Paul started insisting on a date and time as to when he would be able to see her again. I told him I wasn't sure since I didn't have a car. He proceeded to bang on the kitchen counter and eventually knocked off an empty wine bottle onto the floor in one of his rages.

His mother interrupted by saying, "No, Paul, that's enough."

I then started to cry and told his mother I was ready to go.

She said to her daughter, "Sis, let's get Anna." They proceeded to the room to get her and brought her to me. "Come, Maria, I'll walk you to the car," his mother said, trying to console me.

They both started walking me to the car while Paul remained in the kitchen. On my way there, I noticed that

Paul had placed Malaika's (my oldest daughter) handmade blanket at the front door as a doormat. I was so sad and hurt when I saw it that I picked it up quickly and took it with me. His mother and I hugged and said goodbye, and all three of us were crying. I drove off with Anna and felt safe again.

CHAPTER 2

THE ULTIMATE BETRAYAL

I received another telephone message about a week later that Paul wanted to speak with me. This took place after his mother and sister had returned to Jamaica. The message was relayed to me since my whereabouts were still kept secret.

I returned his call about two days later. During the course of our conversation, he was in tears on the phone saying how much he missed Anna and desperately begging me to let him see her. He asked me if he could just take her to the beach for the day and promised to return her to me that evening. Perhaps this might change things, I thought. Maybe he is finally realizing how abusive he's been. I was apt to believe that our separation had taught him a lesson.

I reluctantly agreed to his request, hoping that this would maintain the peace until I could construct a plan to find a new home and file for divorce.

THE WARNINGS

I was now living with Golda's mother who took me into her home for refuge during this awful time. I sought her opinion regarding my intentions to let Anna spend the day with Paul. Her expression was nothing short of disapproval. She reminded me of the times in her house, when Paul verbalized that he would surely take Anna if we ever got divorced. She told me explicitly not to let Paul have her for even a day. She feared that he would disappear with her. I told her I had no intentions of isolating her from her father. She warned me again and left the conversation with an uncomfortable feeling.

Around this same time, I was talking to a very dear friend of mine on the phone who lived in North Carolina. Her name was Corine Jackson, who has now gone on to be with the Lord. We had met in 1976 in Kingston, Jamaica while she was doing mission work there with her husband, Nelson, and we became good friends. When I told her what I was planning to do, she also warned me not to let Paul take AnnaMaria out of my presence. I told her the same thing I told my niece's mother, that it would be unfair of me to prevent him from seeing his child. She insisted that she did not feel good about me allowing Paul to take her anywhere without me. She spoke as one who had a warning from heaven for me. I told her that it was a chance I had to take. I was too overwhelmed with the loss of Malaika and the recent escape. I figured that it would only make matters worse if I restricted him from seeing Anna. Needless to say, I still feared his anger. If I agreed to let him see Anna only in my presence, then I ran the risk of another explosive argument and the possibility of someone being hurt. There was also the risk that he would try to convince me to return to his house, which I had fallen prey to once before. There was still another risk, the risk that those around me seemed to fear the most, as did I. I remembered his threats to take AnnaMaria away if I ever tried to end the marriage. Now I was faced with the risk of his threat becoming a reality, regardless of which option I chose. Nevertheless, I did not heed these warnings.

THE DREADED ENCOUNTER

The moment arrived on July 31st, 1986 at around 2:30 in the afternoon. I arranged to meet Paul at the intersection of 90th Street and Sterling Avenue in Cooper City, Florida,

23

against my better judgment. I chose this type of setting because I did not want to reveal to him where I was staying.

When I arrived at the location where we had decided to meet, he was already there. He came out of his truck and walked towards the car I was driving. He greeted me abruptly and started reaching over to take Anna. I took her out of her car seat and gave her a hug. He then took her out of my arms, said goodbye, and walked away with her towards his Mazda pick-up truck. He mentioned that he would call me later as to a time to return her to me.

I immediately realized that he had left her diaper bag on the front seat of the car I was driving, so I called out to him to get the bag when he suddenly jerked with nervousness. Perhaps he thought I figured out his malicious plans and changed my mind about this beach trip. Despite my hesitations, I walked over to his truck and handed him the bag. Something deep inside my gut made me feel that he was up to something awful. I felt that he was going to run off with her, and I regretted that I had agreed for him to have her for the day.

I went back to the car and watched as he drove off with her and even though I wanted to change my mind, it was too late. ***They were gone***. Little did I know that I would not see her again for the next *five* years and *three* months.

I drove back to my niece's apartment feeling very despondent. I knew in my heart that something was wrong, but I couldn't explain it. I started reflecting on statements Paul had made in the past regarding Anna and what would happen if we were separated or divorced. One of his statements was: "If we get divorced, you know what you will take and what you will leave, because Anna will stay with me." I couldn't help but think that he was going to fulfill that threat now.

A STRANGE FEELING

He called me that evening at my niece's apartment to ask me if Anna could spend the night with him. He agreed to return her the following day. I went along with his request. Then he began to ask me questions about the preparation of her milk formula and some of the other types of food she was allowed to have and how often she should be fed daily. I considered this quite strange since she would be with him for such a short period of time. I hung up the phone expecting to hear from him in the morning and giving him the benefit of the doubt.

He did call about mid-morning on August 1st to see if I was trying to reach him, and I said I wasn't. He called back three more times wanting to know if I was still trying to reach him. Again, I told him no. Then I heard nothing from him for the rest of the evening. The next day, on August 2nd, I tried calling the number he had left with me since I didn't hear from him, but the phone rang without an answer. I waited patiently that whole day and still no call. By now, I was overwhelmed with worry and anxiety.

I started becoming very suspicious that Paul either took off with Anna or was trying to leave the country with her. I immediately called the airport authorities in Miami to see if I could prevent Anna from leaving the country without my permission in case Paul was planning to do so. I was told that a verbal request was not acceptable over the phone. This sort of request, the person explained to me, would require legal documentation and it would entail a process in person. Needless to say, I was very discouraged and disappointed. I felt so desperate, as though my world was slipping through my fingers and I couldn't prevent it from happening.

I then suggested to Golda that we go to the mall for a walk, since I needed to exercise. My due date for delivery was now only six weeks away. About an hour later, we called her husband, Mariano, to see if Paul had called and left a message for me, but there was no message. My heart seemed to sink deeper with fear. I then expressed to my niece that I had this strange feeling that Paul took off with Anna to Jamaica. She tried to console me in her own way, but we were both deeply concerned about Anna's whereabouts. We walked for a little while longer in the mall and then went back to her apartment. There was still no phone call, and my mood had become very solemn.

The long-awaited call came in from Jamaica a few minutes past midnight that threatened my life and instilled the most horrible fear and helplessness in me for years to come. Yet, somehow, I wanted to jump on the plane and go to his mother's house in Jamaica and take my baby by force, but the barriers were obvious. At almost eight months pregnant, no airline would allow me on board given the risk of premature labor. I felt desperate, and my tears seemed endless. Words are inadequate to try and describe how I felt. I now know how some people are capable of doing the unthinkable and then regretting it. It's almost like an invisible cloud that came over me and overshadowed me with instantaneous anxious feelings too desperate to describe. All I could feel at that moment were electric shocks as if it were consuming my stomach. I felt like I was immediately coming unglued. I could hardly breathe. My chest felt like it was beginning to tighten, and my breathing was now being restricted. My head began to throb with excruciating pain so I began to take some deep breaths in an attempt to ease the undue stress I was encountering. I felt like my heart was about to fail. My nerves felt frayed, and I was trembling. In that moment of desperation, I quietly prayed and asked the Lord to help me. I reminded him that He was my only hope. The knowledge of Him was the only restraining force that kept me from doing something absolutely crazy. I remembered reading in the Bible that God promised never to leave us nor forsake us. This was a time when I really needed Him most. I hung on to that promise. I pleaded with him to keep my unborn child safe. After all, He was the giver of life. Immediately, I had to force myself to calm down and tried my best to relax.

The next morning, I went back to Miami where I was staying. I was filled with so much despair and remorse that I had no desire to eat anything. I was so unmotivated and filled with lethargy and fatigue, but Pearline insisted that I eat something for the baby's sake. She soon left for work, and I found myself with a moment of privacy. I decided to call the Silveras to speak with Paul's mother. She came to the phone and informed me that they were preparing for their youngest son's baby dedication. She also mentioned that it was an extremely busy time for her and that she would not be able to speak with me then. I thought it was the most inconsiderate act and one of the coldest responses I had had from her so far, considering the incident with Anna occurred only the night before. The way I felt was, she shouldn't have been too busy to be able to speak with me even for a minute, given what I had just been through. This was the epitome of selfishness. I began to feel anger and the desire for revenge, but somehow I was trapped. The tears were uncontrollable.

At the very least, I needed some sympathy from her. Not only was there no sympathy from her, a mother of five, but she also found it appropriate to brush me off. How would she react if her child were taken? She found no time to speak with me or to console me. Perhaps she didn't want to deal with the issue. The ethical burden of taking a side other than that of her own blood was too much to bear for her. Or, perhaps, she preferred to remain in a state of denial. Enabling her son was far more important at this time than dealing with a potentially hysterical mother who needed to have some answers. I felt so dejected and crushed.

I walked over to Anna's crib and stood there looking at her blanket and her little baby doll she had left behind. She would usually sleep with them. The doll was discolored because she would drag it all over the place with her. Somehow, it didn't get packed in the diaper bag, and it was a small blessing in disguise, because now I had something that was close to her to keep that would remind me of her. I bent over her crib and began to sob uncontrollably. I was almost becoming hysterical. I started having strange pains in my stomach, and then I realized it was from the stress I was encountering. I tried my best to stop crying and to take deep breaths, but it was very hard. I felt the fluttering and rapid movements of the unborn child I was carrying even more now. He was suffering, too. He was absorbing my stress. The signs were evident.

MORE THAN I COULD BEAR

So my older daughter, Malaika, ran away, because she could no longer take the stress of living under the same roof with Paul. AnnaMaria had been abducted by her father and was now in Jamaica. I was almost eight months pregnant with my third child, and I had lost almost everything except for the clothes on my back and a few books. Paul, I found out later, had sold my belongings including my clothes in a garage sale in south Florida.

What did I do wrong? I couldn't help but reflect on the life of Job in the Bible. My life was no parallel to his, but somehow, when suffering enters the arena of one's life, there is the inevitable reflection nonetheless. Had I suffered enough so far in order to give up? Do I curse God and die, as Job's wife had suggested to him? No, I clung closer and cried out to Him for help.

I called my friend, Corine Jackson, in North Carolina, the one who had warned me not to give Anna to Paul, and told her what had happened. This woman was truly a servant of the Lord, and I thought, of course she would tell me what I wanted to hear. She spent much time in prayer and in particular, praying for me. I was crying hysterically when I called her once. She told me she just knew I would call because she was thinking about me so much. She reminded me of her warning to me regarding Anna, and I admitted that I didn't heed it and regretted it very much. She prayed with me, and asked the Lord to help me. I immediately asked her if the Lord had shown her anything concerning my getting Anna back. Her response was no, and that she could not tell me anything unless the Lord had shown it to her. My heart sank.

We kept in touch, and she encouraged me greatly. She was a source of inspiration and counsel for me. She was like my adopted mother. She hated to see me get hurt, and she wanted to help so much. She was more than a true friend; she was my confidante.

MISSED HER 1st BIRTHDAY

It is extremely difficult for me to reflect on this. I choke up with tears even as I write this. I got her a birthday card and wrote the following to *her:*

> *My dearest Anna:*
>
> *Today is your birthday and unfortunately you are in Jamaica with your father who took you away from me against my will and yours. I have sat here and cried all morning just to know you are not with me to even receive a hug or a kiss or to wish you a happy birthday.*
>
> *The cruelty of his act has left me sad, lonely, and very depressed, which is not good considering I'm carrying your little brother or sister who is due to make an entrance into this world anytime. My only prayer at this moment is that the Lord of Heaven will return you to me very soon.*
>
> *Malaika is not here either. Due to your father's unkind treatment of her, she ran away and is now with her father. The pain is more than I can bear knowing that both my children have been taken away from me.*

The only consolation I have at this point is a statement I heard in a movie, which was made by a priest to a little girl whom he loved very much and who suffered a lot of pain, too. He said, "The best is wrought at the cost of great pain."

I hope the pain I've suffered will be the cost for something very good which will include you, Malaika, and the baby.

I love you with all my heart.

Mom

REFLECTIONS

So this was a very sad day for me. I cried most of the day and could hardly eat anything since food had no appeal to me. My head and eyes hurt severely from lack of sleep, and I was so exhausted and extremely distressed. The pain was excruciating and unbearable. I could not take any pain medication to ease my discomfort because of the restrictions of being pregnant. My breathing became more restricted which added to my discomfort. I was feeling so miserable and helpless. I had to bear this intense pain with only occasional ice packs on my forehead. I could feel the persistent throbbing of the blood vessels on both sides of my face. Piercing pains shot through my head like bolts of electricity. Muscles in my body twitched from needed rest. I was so sleep deprived; it was now mind over matter. Exhaustion had taken its full course and deep sleep was far from me. Black circles had enveloped around my eyes, and I felt as if I had been in a war zone. Nothing seemed to suffice or could console me. I was hurting, and I was brokenhearted.

Everything seemed so dark and dreary mentally for me. It felt like I was on a lonely journey, all by myself, and no one understood or was capable of empathizing with me. It felt as if I was dying, and I wanted this journey to end. The only reason I believe I survived those horrible stressful moments was my will and determination to live in order to see my Anna again and my, as yet, unborn child. That was enough to live for, I reasoned. There is no way I could possibly describe the extent of the agony and heartache I was experiencing. There seemed to be no ray or hope, no way out of this dilemma. My hands and feet seemed as if they were to be tied in a knot. No one could fathom the agony of my plight; no one could feel my pain. No one knew the sorrow that I felt in my heart. The only one I believed that knew or understood was the Lord, Jesus. He knew! I could almost feel His consolations at times. There were moments when I felt like He wrapped His arms around me as if to say,

"Don't worry, never mind, I'm going to help you; I've seen the injustice and unkindness that was done to you. Take heart, you will be recompensed." I could almost see His face once more as I did in a dream when I was 14 years old. He seemed so near to me now. His comfort was so real. The knowledge of him was the glue that held me together. It was the balm that soothed my soul. If only He could take me with Him and not let me go through this, I thought. So then I would start uttering quiet prayers to Him appealing and begging for His help. Then I would find myself beginning to weep and my tears would seem to fill many buckets. I felt as if I had shed *thousands of tears* during those days. This would go on day after day, night after night.

"The poor child I am carrying," I thought at times. What stress he was encountering! I could feel his movements that indicated much discomfort. He could feel my pain. Oh, how he suffered. I couldn't help but wonder if he would be okay. I worried about his health at birth. Would he be normal? Would he have problems? I tried my best not to cry at times, but the tears would come rolling down in torrents. My headache would only get worse and the throbbing just seemed to be propelled. Help was no where in sight.

The Florida heat seemed never to leave the nineties in those days. It was so hot and miserable and nothing could console me. Three showers a day didn't seem to suffice. I kept rehearsing the cruelty of Paul's actions over and over in my mind. I thought to myself, no rational human being could do this to another human being considering I was about to have a baby. Did he not care at all whether his second child was born alive, or whether I could have died of stress? No, he was too selfish and thought only of himself to care about us. He didn't care either about disrupting the bonding process between a mother and her 10 month-old baby.

I will never forget when I came home from the hospital with AnnaMaria being only two days old, experiencing the undue stress that a woman's body goes through after giving birth. I was suddenly awakened that night by her crying so I turned to Paul and asked him if he could get the baby from her bed and bring her to me so I could feed her since I was very exhausted. He became angry because he was also awakened from his rest and was so upset that he told me to get her myself. He turned over and ignored me. I couldn't believe what I was hearing.

I dragged myself out of bed, picked her up, and sat in a chair quietly and began to feed her. I was so confused and dismayed and surprised at his attitude and words but most of all, his extremely selfish behavior. My tears began to roll down my cheeks uncontrollably as his mother who was also sleeping in the other room got up and came and stood beside me. She was shocked at his behavior and tried her best to console me and told me to call her if I needed her. After she went back to her room, Paul got up, stood behind me, and began to scold me about wanting pity and just not doing what I was supposed to be doing and that he needed his rest. I kept my mouth closed and intended not to utter a word to him because it would have been futile. Besides, I would have been more upset. He finally walked away and went back to bed. My tears continued quietly to flow. It was such an awful, sad, and lonely time for me instead of it being a happy one.

How could I nurse a child in that state of emotional disturbance? I should have been given help at this point without even having to ask for it. That should have been a given. What husband would refuse to help his wife with a newborn child? I could not fathom his line of reasoning. It was as if his brain was malfunctioning. It was so sad that he complicated, frustrated, and did not appreciate one of the most special and miraculous events in life—that of the birth of his own child. It was inexcusable. Those moments that should have been cherished and valued, were disregarded. He was so unpredictable, so selfish. I cried even more with much remorse and regrets of ever marrying him. What did I get myself into? A lifestyle filled with his selfishness, his controlling and intimidating behavior. How could I have made such a mistake? I regretted now not listening to counsel. I should have taken the things I heard about him seriously. I should never have questioned them. I was now paying the price. It was a big one, too, a precious life was now involved.

I realized that Anna's separation from me could have caused irreparable damage to her emotionally later on. I also knew that the first five years of a child's life were very crucial in terms of emotional and social development. I was now going to be denied those years of nurturing and caring for her. How could this be justified? There was no logical reason for any of this. I would miss all the cute things babies do. I would never hear her first words or get to tuck her in bed at night with a kiss or read her bedtime stories. I would miss seeing her first tooth come in and all the struggles that go along with that. I would never be able to console her or rock her to sleep if she were sick. I would miss the bubble baths and seeing her paint her face with chocolate or ice cream and think it was the most wonderful creation or design. I would miss those peculiar giggles and laughter most toddlers are famous for. I would never see her try to wear my shoes that would be ten times bigger than her little feet, thinking they were hers. I would miss seeing her not having a care in this world or being that little adventurer. She had the makings of it when I last saw her. I could only imagine what it would be like. I know now how much I would miss her hugs and kisses. I would miss getting her dressed and taking her for a walk. Who would be doing these things for her now instead of me?

I would have such a difficult time observing mothers with their toddlers at church, at the mall, or in the supermarkets. I would stare at these little ones trying to envision what my Anna would look like. I wondered about the things she would be able to do at each stage of her development. I would smile at them and comment how cute they were to their moms. Sometimes I would be a bit embarrassed as to how I would stare at them. I would observe them with such endearment. I just wanted to hug them all.

My Pastor's wife, Denise, once said to me, "You can have my Lauren anytime if that would help." Her daughter reminded me so much of my Anna.

No one knew the agony I was going through. I yearned so much to have her with me. I wanted so much to be able to at least see a photograph of her. Nothing could suffice. No one could take her place. She was her own unique little self, and she needed to be with me—not thousands of miles away. I missed her so much. These were the moments that forced me to visit the land of tears, a place I often visited when I encountered such scenes, a place where sorrow lingered and comfort was hard to find. It was a road that led to a lonely place and where no one seemed to care. I felt so overwhelmed, discouraged, and helpless. No one could fathom those agonizing moments except through a similar crisis or through the loss of a loved one. If only I could turn back the hands of time. If only I would not have gone against my better judgment. If only I had not let her out of my sight. Words cannot fully express the emptiness and despair I felt. My nerves were frayed, and my delicate coping skills dangled with uncertainty.

Then it dawned on me that my emotions also would be affected or damaged. I would suffer irreparable harm, too. I would have to fight against the destructive qualities of a dysfunctional life. Yes, I would have to deal with unresolved anger. I would have to draw on all the possible reserves there were to sustain and repair my damaged emotions. Needless to say, depression would hammer its dreary course in me and establish all its end products. Certainly, I would be the one cheated out of enjoying the development of the child God had allowed me to bring into this world. It should be my responsibility to nurture and raise her. After all, she was an extension of me, and I gave her sustenance for nine months. Yes, more importantly, I gave her life, only to have her ripped from my arms. That was cruelty personified!

How could I live with the thought of having my children separated from me? How was I going to explain this to the one who was not yet born? How would I answer his questions? How could I console him as to why his sister was taken away from us? I could not even console myself, much less him. It was not going to be easy.

CHAPTER 3

CUSTODY

I immediately decided to see what help I could get from the state, since I had no money to consult with an attorney. I wouldn't dare call my brother for help since I was mad at him for sending Malaika to Jamaica, so I suffered quietly. I met with a state attorney at the legal aid office in Miami, to see if I could get an emergency injunction approved in order to try and get my child back. She explained to me that custody was an issue and that she was limited in what she could do. She, however, called a friend, Susan Cohen, who was also an attorney in Miami, and asked her if she would help me. Susan agreed to see me and was extremely sympathetic to my situation and told me up front she would not charge me for her services. She was very helpful and was always available for my calls. She was my "saving grace."

We proceeded forth and got an emergency injunction approved, which gave me temporary custody of Anna. In the event Paul entered the country with her, I could take her from him legally. I could not get full custody of both children yet until David was born.

I made many attempts appealing to my ex-husband's family in the hopes of having Anna returned. They mentioned that they had tried, but he would not listen to them. He apparently got into an argument with them concerning her and had left their house with Anna and was staying elsewhere.

In order to get custody, divorce proceedings had to be under way. I agreed to proceed since I had made up my mind based on Paul's behavior. He was notified of such proceedings and was given the opportunity to respond in court in order to have joint custody. There was one prerequisite however, that of returning AnnaMaria to me. Of course, he was not prepared to do that. So, he forfeited his chances of having joint custody.

GO TAKE HER

Almost everyone I had met to this point in the court system was so outraged at what Paul had done. It appeared as if they all wanted to "get him" for me. I remember so well standing before Circuit Court Judge Philip Knight on August 15th,1986, at the time the emergency injunction was approved giving me temporary custody of Anna. I could feel his empathy for me even though I was extremely exhausted, tired, and stressed. He looked straight at me, and by then tears were rolling down my cheeks.

He continued by saying, "Little lady, there is no law in the United States that can protect American citizens that have been taken outside the boundaries of the courts. You are going to have to go take her yourself." So, these words were included in the emergency injunction, and later on in the Final Judgment of Dissolution of Marriage, giving me full custody of Anna. It read:

The Respondent has absconded to Jamaica with the minor, AnnaMaria, without the knowledge or consent of the Petitioner. The Petitioner is authorized as per that order to take AnnaMaria into her custody at once.

I started thinking now that since I have temporary custody perhaps someone at one of these child abduction agencies might help me. I called one that was listed in Perrine, Florida and made an appointment for Monday, August 18th, 1986. I met with a gentleman from the Bureau of Missing Children who told me it would cost a lot of money to get my child back. He didn't give me an exact amount of what it would cost but wanted me to make a down payment before he could get started. I told him I didn't have any money so I left feeling a bit disheartened.

I made another call to the National Center for Missing and Exploited Children in Washington D.C. and explained what had happened with my child. The lady on the other end of the phone told me that since I knew that my daughter was somewhere in Jamaica, she could not help me. In order for them to be able to help me, I could have no knowledge of her whereabouts. She would then be considered a missing child. I was outraged when I heard this.

During one of my conversations with someone in one of the organizations I contacted, I was asked if I had made a police report that my child was taken out of the country without my knowledge. I explained that I had not done that. So, the next morning, I called and reported to the Miami police the fact that my daughter was taken against my will by her father out of the country and an MDPD case #375044G was assigned.

A CHILD IS BORN

I was rushed to the hospital on Sunday, September 14th, 1986, at around 11:30 p.m. that night due to the frequent contractions I was having. It was a little less than a month, just before the divorce was final.

I was placed in a room at Hollywood Memorial Hospital in Pembroke Pines, Florida. Unfortunately, the monitor that I was hooked up to was malfunctioning and the contractions could not be evaluated. I was in a lot of pain so I remained there for the rest of the night, and the contractions were determined to be premature since they petered out completely. I was sent home at around 3:30 p.m. the following afternoon to wait for the "real ones."

On September 19th, 1986, at around 8:00 a.m., I went back to the same hospital with recurring contractions. These were more powerful and lasted much longer. I was placed in another room in a birthing center, and this monitor didn't work either. They decided they were going to move me to another bed but had no idea how much I had dilated.

It was about 11:30 a.m. by this time, and one of the midwives asked me to walk over to another bed where

47

the monitor was working. I didn't think I would make it; I thought I was going to die. I went into the bathroom instead to try and use it when I felt like my entire insides were coming out. I somehow wobbled towards the side of the bed instead and cried out for help. A midwife ran to my rescue and found me leaning sideways on the bed. She took both my legs and gently tried to place them on the bed when she realized that the baby was crowning.

She cried in a desperate voice, "Oh my God, the baby is coming." She appealed to me to push as hard as I could. All I remember was she took a hold of the baby's head and was trying to get him out but there was some difficulty. I heard her whispering, and I didn't know if something was wrong. She kept saying, "You did great! You did great!"

MY LITTLE CONSOLATION ARRIVED

So at 12:00 noon, David Alexis made his entrance into this world. He was immediately rushed off to the nursery for observation. I found out later that the umbilical cord was wrapped around his neck three times, and he was choking. He was being monitored the whole day, and I couldn't see him until the next morning.

When I saw him, his little eyes were bruised and swollen, and I realized then that God had spared his life.

He was a miracle child. I decided then I would name him David, which means "Beloved of God." For a middle name, I thought I would call him Alexis, which in Greek means, "a helper." I realized that he was all I had now, and one day he would become my helper. I held him and wept. "My little consolation" had arrived.

The Lord then reminded me of a dream I had when I was about seven months pregnant with David. In that dream, *I had given birth to this little baby boy. When he was about six months old we were in a room with some other people. It seemed like it was a church function of some kind. All of a sudden, this baby, who was mine and who was not able to stand on his own yet, stood up on a chair and began to speak these incredible things. He appeared to be a prophet. I remembered he was wearing cloth diapers.* It's funny, but that's what he wore because I couldn't afford pampers. The Lord revealed before he was born that I would have a boy, and I did. A truly special child he has been. He played a key role in later developments.

AT THE MERCY OF THE STATE

It then dawned on me that I was perhaps the only mother there on that hospital ward that had no husband coming to see his wife and newborn baby. We were instead at the mercy of the state, merely surviving. I would rather have died than to endure the previous twenty-four hours of lonely torture. I thought there was no one on the face of this earth who could comprehend the depth of grief and sorrow I experienced at that moment. It is not easily described. There I was, lying in a state maternity ward, my body traumatized by childbirth, my mind more fragile than eggshells, and my heart in a thousand pieces. It was I who suffered now, as my ruthless husband and his well-to-do family in Jamaica were content in their selfishness. Not a penny in support of their newest namesake.

I remembered the Jamaican nurse who came into my room to check my chart and take my temperature. She looked at me, called me by name, and then looked at the name on the chart again. Why the puzzled look on her face? Did she recognize the name from the billboards in Jamaica? Was I supposed to be in different circumstances? Shouldn't I have been able to afford insurance instead of being at the mercy of the state? Surely my manner of speech and look did not match up in her eyes with my circumstances. Something was wrong. She was not about to pry, however. She knew how people with the word "state" written on their charts were treated. They were ignored for long periods of time. She wasn't going to take that chance; she didn't know who she had in her care. She was very polite and gentle with me. She saw that I wasn't speaking much, and from the fact that no husband appeared, she was convinced now that there was definitely a problem. She always addressed me as Mrs. Silvera, as is customary in Jamaica. I found it curious, since the culture in South Florida was much more informal, even in professional environments. Who knows what she was thinking. One thing she knew for sure was that I needed comfort and support. We were released from the hospital when David was breathing normally and was given a clean bill of health by the doctor. We spent a total of two and a half days there.

During this time, Paul's parents were traveling on a world cruise and called my friend's house in Miami and left a telephone message for me, inquiring if "the baby" was born. They figured I would get the message somehow. I was so hurt from their previous behavior that I had no desire to speak with them. Their message indicated that they would try to call again, but they didn't. I was advised by my attorney to channel any form of communication with them through her office. They chose not to cooperate.

About a week after we returned to the house where we were staying, the Silveras called again and found out that David was born. Now that I had been contacted, it was time to change my location in case Paul came looking for me. He had also called one night, and I just happened to pick up the phone without thinking; I usually screened the calls. He told me that he did not intend to live without his son. He also said I had the option to come to Jamaica and join him. If not, I would always be looking over my shoulders because he would send for David. I slammed the phone in his ears and had no further conversations with him for several months.

MY SECRET WEAPON

So on October 22nd, 1986, the divorce was finalized, and I was granted full custody of AnnaMaria and David. However, somehow, I was being plagued with mixed emotions. I felt relieved and free, yet, I felt so sad and lonely. Although, I thought I wouldn't have to spend Valentine's Day crying because of some insults that would be hurled at me instead of getting roses or, wondering if I would be hurt physically for not answering some stupid question I was asked. I didn't have to worry about calling a police officer and having him go back with me to the house in order to warn Paul that if he did hit me he would be imprisoned. I wouldn't have to hear him scream at Malaika to go to bed at 8:30 p.m. while she was trying to finish her homework or study for a test.

Never again would I have to hear these insensitive, mindless words being reiterated to me or reverberating in my ears: **"You will suck salt through a wooden spoon."** In other words, I would suffer, and he would not help. Time proved him wrong, however, the God of Heaven saw to it.

I felt as if I had a secret weapon now. Just how it would be used, I didn't know. All I knew was that this judge seemed fair and sympathetic and was trying his best to help me. He knew how inadequate the law was then and what the limits were. He somehow saw my agony and helplessness. I liked his approach; he did his best. He had a heart! May God bless him!

A PLACE TO LAY OUR HEADS

My friend Stella and her husband, Arthur, agreed for us to come and stay with them. They also lived in Miami. They loved David very much and were very helpful to us. I remember shortly after we moved in with them that David started showing signs of distress. He would cry hysterically at times and whimper intensely. His little body seemed to vibrate. I started becoming worried and didn't know what to do. I would hold him up on my shoulders at 2:00 and 3:00

a.m. and walk about with him until he would stop crying. Of course, I wasn't getting much sleep.

On one occasion, Stella came into the room early one morning and said to me, "Let us agree to pray that the Lord will heal this child from all the stress he has been through."

We both prayed, believing that God would intervene and calm David's little body. Well, He heard our prayers and the whimpering and shaking stopped. I was very glad for that.

I did my best to cope, given the circumstances. I would go to bed at night and cry most times. I was also hurting physically from muscle strains and the postpartum depression many women encounter after giving birth. I was barely coping. I suffered from severe back and neck aches, not to mention tension headaches that plagued me day and night. There was no rest for the weary. There was also no time to focus on myself because I had a helpless child to care for. I had to figure out how we were going to buy food, clothes, and simply survive.

I took David for his six-week check-up, and the nurse we saw at the clinic enquired about my delivery. When I told her what had transpired she turned to me and said, *"Honey, this child had to live."*

I thought that was very interesting. I knew God had preserved his life and this was a confirmation.

On November 16th, 1986, David Southwell of Christian Faith Fellowship in Miami dedicated little David to the Lord. He was almost two months old. He was surely the source of my happiness in those days. Going to church with him and thanking God each week for sparing our lives was a major light in my life. His life being such a miracle was evident before me everyday.

A MOMENT OF DESPERATION

A friend of mine, who was an attorney in Kingston, Jamaica, was visiting Miami and came by to see us. I asked her if she could try and find out if Anna was still at the Silveras' when she returned to Jamaica. She agreed she would try to find out for me. At that moment, desperation moved me. I actually asked her if something could be arranged like paying some guys to scale the fence at the Silveras' house and be prepared to shoot the dogs if necessary to try and get Anna. She realized by then that I was getting a bit unrealistic, so she quite calmly said she would not recommend my suggestion. She explained further to me that based on her past experiences in the courtroom, fathers like Paul do not give up easily in those kinds of instances and are extremely obsessive in their behavior. Anna, she emphasized, could be seriously hurt in the process. In some cases, she explained, the father destroyed himself and the child before he would give in or give up the child. That scared me enough for Anna's safety that I promptly did away with that idea in a hurry. I would not jeopardize her life for my desperate ambition. Instead, I would prefer to live without her than to know that she could be hurt and could possibly die as a result of my emotional response. This situation now required objective thinking on my part, an approach that would not only involve my interests but her welfare, as well. It was a hard decision to make but nonetheless the right one.

CHAPTER 4

TOO CLOSE FOR COMFORT

David was now four months old, and I was long overdue for a reprieve. The fatigue and exhaustion from raising an infant alone was reaching its peak. I decided to go home to my mother's house in Jamaica. I was a bit scared, however, that Paul would find me there and attempt an abduction of his son, David. I called my mother and told her of my plans, and she said not to worry but to come on home. We flew into Montego Bay in January of 1987 and stayed there for about three months.

My mother was happy to see David again. She had traveled to Miami about a week after he was born to help me. She was a blessing in disguise.

I started to relax and was now beginning to thaw out. The beautiful sunshine and coconut water were like good medicines for us, and I was also getting much needed rest. I took David to the beach regularly, and he thoroughly enjoyed the water. I was still very cautious, however, and looked around me constantly just in case of any suspicious characters. Paul's younger brother was an airline pilot who flew locally so I avoided that part of the airport. I wouldn't take any chances of being seen. The risks were too great. Could I stand the thought of losing David also, given prior threats? I felt like a stranger in my own hometown.

Malaika was now settled in an excellent high school in Kingston, about 4 hours away by car. She came to visit us at Carondel Hill in Montego Bay, our family home, where she once lived with my mother and I before life took such a terrible roller-coaster turn. This was her first time seeing David, and she fell head over heels for him. She wanted to do everything she could to take care of him, play with him, and feed him. It was as if she was with AnnaMaria back in Florida again. Her visit was short since she was in school, but we made the most of the time we had together. It was difficult to say goodbye again, but I had agreed for her to stay in Jamaica to finish high school. She was attending Immaculate Conception, a private Catholic high school, whose academic standards were outstanding. I was pleased with the caliber of education she was receiving.

About a month later, the first week in March, my sister, Nicky, who lived there, asked me if I could take her vehicle and transport her house guest to this ocean front restaurant. He was an investor in this project. His name was David, a Jewish businessman from New York. He was eighty years old at the time and had more spunk than a forty-year-old person. He was full of life and had lots of energy. He most certainly could outrun me!

I arranged to pick him up at about 10:00 a.m. He was ready and waiting when I arrived. I asked him in a joking way if he was ready for his safari ride since I was driving a jeep. He said he was game. We had a good laugh and started on our journey.

I mentioned that I was visiting my family and that I also had a David. He wanted to know if I had any more children. I told him yes and that unfortunately my ten-and-a-half-month-old daughter was taken without my permission by her father and was in Kingston as we spoke and that he had threatened to kill me if I ever tried to get her back.

He became very quiet for a moment and then said, "I will not sit back as an American and see this injustice take place with another American." He continued to say, "I'm

59

sure an old friend would not mind doing me a favor. In fact, he owes me a few." He added, "We will go to Kingston and meet with him. All expenses will be paid by me."

U.S. AMBASSADOR LENDS AN EAR

Two days later, on March 9th, we flew to Kingston where we were met at the airport by the chief of police, a gracious man. He transported us to the office of the United States Ambassador to Jamaica and later picked us up. Both men greeted each other being former acquaintances from New York. I was then introduced to the ambassador at which point he inquired about my surname, Nicholas, the maiden name that I assumed after the divorce. He recognized it was Greek and that we had something in common, both our fathers were from Cyprus.

He listened very attentively to my story and was very sympathetic. However, he informed me that there was nothing he could do personally to help me and that I needed to speak with the American consul based at the American embassy in Kingston. He was far more familiar with such matters and would be the one to consult. Besides, he was knowledgeable with both American and Jamaican laws. If anyone could lend insight or assistance, he would be the one. The ambassador subsequently called the U.S. consul and informed him that we would be on our way shortly to see him.

At the American embassy, we met with the U.S. consul and poured over Anna's case in detail. He was most helpful and suggested that I first get a warrant from the State of Florida before he could attempt any proceedings in Jamaica. He gave me his business card with his direct office telephone number and told me I could call him anytime if I had any questions. I realized then that I had a mission to pursue once I returned to Florida.

BACK TO REALITY

Our stay in Jamaica went very well, and we had no encounters with Paul. I would have liked to stay longer and forget my problems, yet I knew that a process awaited me. Psychologically, I was not prepared for it. The unknown scared me a bit, too. On top of all that, I would have to find a job as soon as possible to be able to support us since there was no child support.

Our little vacation ended in Montego Bay, and we arrived in Florida about the first week in April. Shortly after that, I contacted the pastor of Christian Faith Fellowship in Miami, to let him know that we were back and also that I was looking for a job. He told me that he needed someone to help out in the front office of the church and that I could start working immediately if I wanted.

Now that I had secured a job, I decided to make an appointment to see an officer in the Cooper City Police Department to get the process started. I was referred however to the Federal Bureau of Investigation to see what could be done regarding my case. I met with a special agent who investigated as much as he could but explained that the process of a warrant had to be handled by the police department. He therefore referred me back to Cooper City Police. A detective sergeant was then assigned to my case. He got all the information he needed from me and presented my case before the state attorney's office. The warrant was denied on the basis that custody was not established when Paul took Anna, and therefore, he had as much right to her as I did.

I relayed the information I received from the detective to the U.S. consul in Kingston. He was a bit disappointed but informed me in a letter and also over the phone, that he had had some discussions with the Deputy Director of Public Prosecution for Jamaica, who had direct control of all extradition cases. He explained that without a warrant charging Paul with an offense, there could clearly be no extradition. Besides, it would have to constitute an offense under Jamaican law.

He made two suggestions: Either I bring an action for divorce and custody in Jamaica or I look into the possibility of the Jamaican courts granting comity, that is recognition to my Florida divorce and custody decree. This would be similar to going through a divorce proceeding in Jamaica. The deputy admitted that he didn't think that would be successful, and neither did I. I thanked the U.S. Consul for his help and continued working with the Cooper City Police.

I realized that in order to go to work I would need a sitter for David. I was very fortunate to have someone referred to me. Claudette was originally from Trinidad. She loved David like her own child and took excellent care of him. I was very thankful for that. At least I didn't worry about him during the days. He was very happy with her, and her two boys helped to entertain him when they came home from school. So I started my job at Christian Faith Fellowship around the first part of May.

I continued my communication with the detective in the Cooper City police office. He filed my case a second time with the state attorney's office, and it passed on one level but was turned down at the final stage. Even though the case was approached from the angle that Paul schemed and masterminded a plan to take Anna, custody was the issue. My case was not approved, and I could not get a warrant for Paul's arrest in order to take Anna. Needless to say, I was very disappointed in the outcome and ended up writing a letter expressing my feelings of disappointment to the state attorney's office that was handling the case.

All the while, I had been calling a few more organizations including the Adam Walsh Foundation in Florida, but the response was the same, either they could not help me or no one returned my call. I was becoming increasingly discouraged.

THE DREAM I HELD ON TO

I kept praying throughout all this that the Lord would help me to be able to get back Anna. I had friends praying for me also. *One night however, in late August of 1987, I dreamt that I got her back. I was trying to find the detective to tell him, but I couldn't find him. As the dream continued, Anna and I were sitting on this bench, and I was starring at her because she was so beautiful. She had a mass of dark gorgeous curls and big black eyes that were looking straight into mine. Then she said, "Mommy, I love you." I responded to her by saying, "Darling, I love you."* What

I realized had taken place in the dream was that God had healed the years that were lost between us, but I couldn't explain it to anyone. It just happened in the dream. *When she smiled at me, it was as if nothing had happened as far as us being apart for over five years.* It's interesting, but this dream took place in 1987 and I got her back in 1991. She was six years old when I got her back and that was the age she was in the dream. God is so accurate and faithful. He revealed to me what she would look like when I got her back and what he was going to do.

CHAPTER 5

INVITED TO THE BALL

By this time, David and I were in a two-bedroom apartment in Cooper City, Florida. My mother had also come to spend some time with us from Jamaica, to help out with taking care of David. She kept him during the days while I was at work, and it was such a treat to come home in the evenings to a cooked meal. She had spoiled us with her delicious Jamaican home-cooking and enjoyed her role as grandma at the same time. She taught David the secrets of playing hide and seek but made sure she would seldom be found. She was a life-saver.

David was now about fourteen months old when I received a call from my friend David Buntzman in New York. He was inviting me to attend the annual Friends

67

of Jamaica Ball to be held on November 14th, 1987 at the Waldorf Astoria Hotel in New York. This was a fundraiser for Jamaica, and David was certain that the prime minister of Jamaica would be in attendance. He felt that this would be an excellent opportunity for me to seek his support in Anna's case. I was excited and wanted very much to attend. David mentioned that if I could get to New York, all my expenses would be taken care of. I told him I would get back to him.

In conversation one morning, I mentioned what David had told me to my employer. To my surprise, he offered to pay my way to New York because he knew I would not have been able to afford the airfare. I accepted his offer and was very grateful for his help. I then called David and informed him of my plans. He was delighted to know that I had planned to attend the function in New York and told me he would make the necessary arrangements. I told my mother what had transpired, and she realized that I needed a dress for the occasion so we went shopping, and she bought me an outfit.

The moment came, and I arrived in New York. I was on a mission to try and get my daughter back. I would not leave a single stone unturned. If a door was open, I would walk through it. I was determined to explore every possibility that was placed before me. So far, nothing was really working. Could this be my moment?

David picked me up from the airport and made sure I got checked in at the Barbizon Hotel where he had made arrangements for me to stay. He then took me to meet a Greek friend of his who would escort me to the opera since we had some time to spare. The weather at that time of the year was beautiful. The air was crisp and very inviting for strolling and window shopping. We had a wonderful afternoon and ended up having cappuccino at a sidewalk cafe before our time was up. I took a taxi back to the hotel to get ready for the ball, and David was on time, as expected, to pick me up. Off we went to the Waldorf Astoria.

We arrived at our destination, and I felt like "Cinderella at the Ball." This hotel was so breathtaking. The architecture and décor was stunning. I had never seen a hotel more exquisite. Everyone we saw upon entering was elegantly dressed. I felt out of place because my dress could not be compared to theirs in terms of monetary value. Yet, to me, mine did suffice since I was there on a mission and not to impress anyone. If David approved, that was enough.

His plan for me was to meet the prime minister of Jamaica since he knew him personally. He also thought that if the opportunity presented itself, I could discuss the situation of my daughter with him. He got his bit of coaching in with me of course, and he emphasized that unless I had the ear of the prime minister, I should not bring up the subject. His reason for this was because there would be so many people there who would be trying to socialize and make acquaintances with him. The prime minister then would not be able to focus on my problem given the many distractions he would face. I was also bothered by the fact that my former husband knew the prime minister and that this could possibly work against me. I was therefore faced with the unknown. The question now was: How do I approach the subject?

We made our way up the elevator to the floor where a reception was being held. David pointed out the prime minister to me even though I had met him once before at a party at his house in Jamaica. David said to me at that point, "Anyone in this room has access to Mr. Seaga."

I pondered for a few moments, as my mind was developing a strategy. "I'm going to take a picture with him," I announced.

"Go ahead," he replied.

I took a deep breath and smiled at David as I moved off from our area. I walked slowly and gingerly toward the prime minister. I knew my every move was being noted, as his secret service men were all standing in the background.

"Mr. Prime Minister, may I have my picture taken with you?" He gave an affirmative nod and turned to one of the men behind him. It was a secret service agent who snapped away with the camera, taking a few good shots.

The prime minister then turned and greeted me and wanted to know if I lived in New York. I explained that I was living in Florida, and then he wanted to know what had brought me to New York. I mentioned that a friend had invited me to attend the function. "Now, Maria! This is the moment!" I said to myself.

I knew I had his attention, as David had mentioned. Somehow I just didn't bring up the subject of Anna in time. Within a few seconds, we were interrupted by someone, and I backed away, returning to speak with David. My golden moment was gone in a flash.

There were perhaps a thousand people in attendance. They were from all walks of life. Some were dignitaries representing different countries and others were local friends and loyal supporters of this annual event. Regardless of fame or fortune, this was going to be an evening that would be well spent.

We moved into the ballroom where the dinner was being served. We sat at a table next to the British ambassador to the United Nations and his wife. David got up shortly after we were seated and started visiting with some old friends. The ambassador and his wife introduced themselves along with the others at the table, and everyone became acquainted. After the meal was over, the music continued to play and people started dancing. I had decided that I was not here to dance. My mind was elsewhere.

Then the ambassador turned to me and said, "Would you like to dance?"

My response was "No, not really."

He chuckled and said, "I've never seen a Jamaican that didn't like to dance, shall we?" He proceeded to take my hand and off we went for a waltz. I must admit it was fun, and that he kept me on my toes. One could tell he attended his ballroom lessons faithfully.

The evening seemed to have sped along. It was now around 11:00 p.m., and David was ready to leave. He told me he was going to say goodbye to the prime minister, so we walked over to where he was sitting.

David greeted him and said goodbye, and he shook my hand and said, "You're leaving already?"

To which I replied, "Yes, my Cinderella time is up."

He chuckled and said goodbye. Again, I could have interjected to ask him about Anna, but it just did not feel like the right time to mention anything.

On the way back to my hotel, David and I discussed the evening. We realized that I did not get to present my problem to the prime minister. However, he assured me that it was not all in vain and that I could now attempt to meet with him in Jamaica at which time he would remember me and would be able to give more time to the matter. David had a strategy. It's that old wisdom, I suppose.

A few weeks later, I went over to the home of two of my friends who also attended our church, Percy and Sybil. They were also from Jamaica. Percy worked at the Jamaican Embassy in Miami. His wife, Sybil, suggested that we write a letter to him and see what his response would be regarding Anna. We drafted the letter and sent it to him, and he responded to it by saying that he did not want to get involved in such a personal family affair. That ended my quest for the prime minister's help.

CHAPTER 6

THE PROWLER

By September of 1988, my daughter was now two years old. Although my quest continued, there seemed to be no leads. I had to march through life without her, as painful as that was.

Work was going well when I received a message from a friend informing me that Paul was in Miami and that he had left a telephone number for me to call him. I thought about it and called him back later on that morning from a payphone and spoke with him for my entire lunch time. I basically appealed to him to return Anna, so he could have access to both his children but he would not agree to do so. He kept saying that I would not allow him to see Anna again if he returned her. I assured him I would, and I sincerely meant it. I also remembered saying to him that what he had done was morally and ethically wrong, and it would backfire on him if he chose not to set things right. He kept insisting on seeing David. I told him the only way he would see David was if he agreed to return Anna. I mentioned to him also that I could meet him with the authorities at an agreed location in the event he was willing to abide by my terms. Instead, he started crying on the phone and told me it was hard for him to return her. He nevertheless stuck to his position and refused to cooperate. I, too, feared for my little David. I could not risk bringing him right into Paul's presence. In my mind, this was not only about fearing the worst, but about facing the inevitable. Paul would surely have taken his only son by force, given the chance. There was nothing that would persuade me to make that gullible mistake again. The conversation ended in gridlock; no Anna for me, no David for him.

A NARROW ESCAPE

Paul returned to the United States again in the early part of December of 1998. This time, he called me at the office, and I was shocked to find out that he had my telephone number at work. I found out later that someone I knew had given him the number. He had the person fully convinced that I should to let him see David. What he concealed from the person was his intention to snatch David from me, too. His prior statement to me reverberated in my mind, "I will not live without my son."

About a month before his recent trip to Miami, I had a dream that *Paul was stooped down outside my apartment door. He was hiding from me and didn't want me to know he was there. When I opened the door, I saw him and I was scared because I knew he would snatch David so I closed the door quickly.* I woke up from the dream terrified and startled.

Well, once I knew he was in town, I called my friend Corine in North Carolina that evening and told her. I also told her the dream I had and that I was scared. I mentioned that Lily, my friend, offered for us to come and stay with her until I knew Paul had left the country.

She said to me, "Maria, what are you waiting for? God has already warned you in the dream. Get out of there and go to your friend's place!" I called Lily immediately and told her I was coming over. I quickly packed a few things and left my apartment that night, with David clutched to my side.

I made it to Lily's house safely. I was gripped with fear the whole way. I thought somehow Paul was going to jump out from somewhere at us. That night, while sleeping at Lily's house, I had another dream. I dreamt that *I barely got out of my apartment, hurried into my car, and drove off, when I suddenly realized from looking in my rearview mirror, that Paul was behind us in a car racing to try and catch us, but he never did.* Again, I awakened with the most petrified feeling.

The next morning at work, my boss answered the phone while I was out on an errand. Paul wanted to know if I had come to work since I was not at home the night before. He told him that I was just not in at the moment. I called my niece to tell her I would not be home for a few days since she occupied the apartment below mine. She asked me if I had a visitor the night before. I told her that I was not there. She said she heard some footsteps going up the stairs by my apartment at about 11:00 p.m. that night, but she did not look to see who it was. Paul knew I was not at home! He must have gone there looking for me but could not find me. The Lord was my shield and protector.

Later on that month, I was told that the church was experiencing some financial difficulties, and that they would no longer be able to keep me on. I was forced to give up my apartment, put my things in storage, and move in with my friends Phil and Lily. Their friendship was so loyal, and their support for David and me was unwavering.

AN ENCOUNTER OF THE WORST KIND

While staying with my friends, I received another message sometime in late December that Paul was trying to reach me again. I kept the number he left and called it a few days later and spoke with him. Of course, he was still trying to be able to see David, but I would not agree to his terms. "Once bitten, twice shy," goes the old expression. I made one last attempt to appeal to him to return Anna but he would not listen.

Lying there on Lily's sofa, I was thinking about the fact that I was now out of a job, and the stress of it all started getting to me. So, the headaches started again, and this particular one was pretty bad. It prevented me from going on a walk with David and Lily. So I decided to have a hot cup of tea and relax while they both took off with David on his tricycle.

About twenty five minutes after they had left, Lily came running back into the apartment with David, all flustered and hysterical, saying she had just seen Paul in a red truck in the complex where we were. She had seen pictures of him prior to this, so she recognized him. I immediately asked her if he saw when she entered her apartment. She said no. My head started pounding even more nevertheless, thinking that he might show up at the door. Needless to say, we were consumed with this for the rest of the evening. We decided that we must try and figure out if Paul was really staying in the same complex where we were. How else could he get past this gated community unless he had a card to get in or gained entrance through the guard at the gate? Even in a "secure" neighborhood, we still were not safe from his terror.

THE DISGUISE

When Phil, Lily's husband, came home from work that evening, we got his approval to drive their van that night around the complex in the hope of finding the red truck. Lily and I had this brilliant idea of disguising ourselves so as not to be recognized. Since Phil was a fireman, we decided to borrow his hat. Lily wore it, and I wore a straw hat. We were set to go. Phil watched David, and we sneaked out at around 10:30 p.m. If someone had said "boo" to us, we would have collapsed on the ground. We were so scared we were going to get caught.

Anyway, we drove around the entire complex and saw no sign of the truck. Then Lily said, "Let's go down this road, we haven't been there yet." Sure enough, there was the truck, parked outside one of the apartments on 13th Court. We wrote down the license plate number and the apartment number. Mission accomplished; we had obtained our clues.

We went back to the house filled with excitement because we had found the red truck. The problem now was, I had to be careful going in and out of the complex for fear of being seen by Paul. He was so sneaky, that no one could tell whether or not he was lurking around just watching in case he spotted me. We were extremely cautious. We were always looking behind us in case we were being followed. We also double-checked the cars in front of us upon entering the complex to make sure we didn't see the red truck.

The next day, I decided to call the telephone number Paul had left to see if he was still around. I wanted to know if he was really the person Lily saw in the complex. I also wanted to be able to describe some of the landmarks close by to see if he was actually in the vicinity. I first thought I would throw him off by asking if he was driving in an area where he was not seen by Lily. So, I asked him if he was driving a red truck on University Drive in Plantation and also if he was wearing a cap. He admitted to both things. I just wanted to confirm what Lily had seen. Then he volunteered to give me some information of what happened on his way over to the C.B. Smith Park area. He said he saw this lady walking a little boy who looked like David, and he stopped her and asked her if his name was David, and she said "no," so he continued driving. He then said he was driving near the C.B. Smith Park area and he saw this other Chinese lady with a little boy that he thought looked just like David. He slowed down and looked at him and almost asked her if his name was David, but he didn't because he thought he made a fool of himself with the first lady so he didn't want to ask her his name a second time. He kept driving instead. That was exactly what Lily described to me—a man with a cap in a red truck slowed down looked at David and drove off. Also, Lily is Chinese. The pieces were connecting. We decided to lie low and limit our outside activities. However, later one afternoon, Lily and I went by the Cooper City Police office and reported our findings.

Meanwhile, Paul's mother was passing through town and left a message along with a telephone number for me to call her. I returned her call, and she asked me if I would come and see her along with David. I said I would, only if she could guarantee me that there would be no "baggage" with her, meaning Paul. She assured me there would be none. So we met and had dinner while Paul was in town. This was her first time seeing David.

Well, Paul's intentions of trying to snatch David fell through, and he left for Germany in early January of 1989 to join AnnaMaria whom he had sent there previously with his new-found German bride whom he married in Jamaica.

I discovered that Paul had obtained a Jamaican passport and citizenship for AnnaMaria. This was how she was able to travel to Germany. He was so proud of his accomplishments that he mailed me a copy of the final documents for my records. My hopes now of seeing Anna were becoming dimmer, and I was starting on a very lonely journey to try and get her back.

CHAPTER 7

STARTING ALL OVER AGAIN

One Sunday evening, I decided to take David for a stroll in the Broward Mall because we were a bit housebound. After walking around for a while and feasting our eyes, I decided to call Diana, a girlfriend, to say hello. She had recently relocated to Ft. Lauderdale from Jamaica, and I had not seen her since she had been living there. During the course of our conversation, she inquired where we were and then asked me if we would like to come for dinner at her house. I agreed and she gave me directions.

After dinner, I mentioned to Diana that I was looking for a job and that she should keep her ears opened in the event she heard of anything. Just then her friend, Betty, dropped in on her way for a walk. She mentioned to Betty that I was looking for a job and that she should let us know if she knew of anything. Betty said she would mention it to her husband, Don, because she thought he was looking for someone for the front office. I eventually met Don, a self-styled businessman who hired me two weeks later on February 1st, 1989. I ended up working ten years for his company. He was a great employer and a very generous person. He and Betty became my good friends.

While in this job, I did my best to fight depression and stress. By now, I was severely affected physically. I would get such terrible migraines. I also suffered from chronic constipation. This was all due to stress. Many of my lunch times were spent lying flat on my back in a small catalog room with the lights off just to try and ease the pain along with a few Excedrin.

I commuted to work for a while until I saved enough money to rent an apartment. I eventually found one in Pine Island Ridge, a beautiful community. David and I really enjoyed living there. It was great for bike-riding and taking walks.

About a year after we were living at Pine Island Ridge, I received a call from the detective at the Cooper City Police office about the first part of 1990. I thought he had good news for me, but instead, he told me the FBI was not interested in my case! My heart felt a bit of stress, but by now, I was getting used to doors being closed. Disappointments for me were now becoming a way of life. I was spiraling down with discouragement.

YOU CAN'T GIVE UP

One evening, after coming home from work, I was so tired that David and I fell asleep on the sofa curled up together. The phone rang and woke us up. It was my older daughter, Malaika, who was in college at the University of Wisconsin. She wanted to know if I had received any news about Anna, so I told her what the detective had told me. I also said that I was getting very weary and tired and that I could not fight anymore; I was about to give up.

She started almost screaming at me saying, "No, Mommy, you can't give up on Anna! You deserve to raise her, not Paul. Anna will be all messed up if she lives with him. Besides, if you don't go after Anna now, while she is young, she will eventually find you. She will ask you why you gave her up."

I told her I didn't know what I was going to do but right now I was weary. She tried her best to encourage me, but I was so disheartened that it seemed like her voice was faint in my mind. I listened as best as I could, given my emotional state at that time. Our relationship was now on the mend, and Malaika wanted so much for me to be reunited with Anna, for my sake, and for Anna's sake.

PRAYERS, LITTLE ONES AND BIG ONES

By this time, David was about three and a half years old, and he loved looking at pictures in our photo albums. One day, he discovered a picture of Anna and me. He stared at it for quite some time before inquiring of me who she was. When I told him she was his sister, he wanted to know where she was and declared that he wanted to play with her.

My heart sank because I had not prepared an explanation that would be adequate for my son. Why was she not living with us? The answer for Malaika was simple: she was in college. There was no easy explanation for Anna's absence. I had not been challenged by my little boy to explain any of the family dynamics before now, as he was still young and unaware. Now that family relationships were meaningful in his developing mind, I realized I would have to find a way for not only me, but also David, to cope.

My response to him was, "Darling, let's just pray and ask Jesus to help us get Anna back."

He did not question my motive but always wanted us to pray that she would come and be with us. One night after we read our Bible story, his prayer went like this: "Jesus, I ask you to bring my sister back so I can have her to play with."

He was very serious, and he prayed the same prayer for several nights, then on and off. A few months later, while we were praying, his prayer went like this: "Jesus, you're not answering my prayer. You haven't brought my sister back yet."

I thought to myself, this child is very serious. He knows and believes what he is praying.

We met on several occasions for prayer at the home of a friend by the name of Joanne Biernacki. David would come out of the room where he was playing by himself, and he would wait for his turn to pray. We would hear this little voice from behind the sofa saying, "Jesus, I ask you to bring my sister back so I can have her to play with." He would then walk back into the room and start playing again.

I am convinced that God hears the prayers of little ones, and He answers them. I've always said that if no other prayer was answered regarding Anna, God heard David's prayer for his sister.

One day, my friend Judy said to me, "You know, Maria, we need to keep praying for Anna's return. We are just going to believe for the day when we have her back with us."

I decided I would use my lunch time once or twice a week, and we would meet at her house and pray at that time since our lives were so busy. She home-schooled her girls, and the lunch hour was a good break for her. We met regularly and prayed for about fifteen or twenty minutes each time, then I returned to work. We did this for about six months.

THE PRAYER GROUP

Later that year, Judy mentioned to me that her friend Joanne had started a prayer group, and she would like me to be a part of it. The group met for the first time in April of 1990, and I joined them shortly after that. There were nine of us altogether who started out with this group: Joanne, Ursula, Judy, Indira, Gloria, Eunice, Bob, Vera, and me. Later on, Gary, Joanne's husband, joined us. We met every Wednesday at noon. I continued to use my lunch time to meet with them for forty-five minutes. We would also be fasting each time we met. We had many prayer requests in the group, but we always remembered to pray for Anna's return. We asked the Lord to perform a miracle and bring her back. It was so empowering to have a support group like that who encouraged and prayed for each other. Many scriptures of promises were given to me from the members of the group. I kept them and read them continually. They were a wonderful source of encouragement for me, too.

MY PACT WITH GOD

I continued praying and asking God to help me because nothing else seemed to work. My depression became so overwhelming at times that I thought I would not make it to the next day. I had now been diagnosed with a herniated disc in the right side of my neck. It was very painful, and life was getting more miserable with the severe headaches I was having.

David was the angel who kept me going. One night, after I had put him to bed, I started listening to some music by Hosanna, a time of consolation for me. This was the only time I could just sit and relax without being inundated with things to do. The particular tape I was listening to was entitled *In His Presence*. My mind started reflecting on God's infinite wisdom and all that He had created, and it dawned on me that my problem was so finite to Him that if I would only put into practice what His Word said about believing and having faith in Him without doubting, then I should have my request.

So, I became bold. Next, I stepped out on my deck and began to be in a serious intercessory, prayerful mode. I meant business tonight. This was about 12:30 a.m. I looked over onto the lake in front of me and then looked up into the heavens and saw the stars; they were so beautiful. Then I thought to myself: "God, you are so awesome to design all this." By then, I started crying and found myself saying out loud:

> *"If you created the heavens, the earth, the animals, and man in relation to all that, then this is not too difficult for you to do. I will not give up until you bring Anna back."*

I then fell on my face in the living room where the music was playing and just cried out to God. My tears flowed and flowed. Some were from deep regrets of marrying Paul and the havoc he had created in my life, and the others were wishing and hoping that things would change. I stayed there for about another hour listening to my music and reflecting on all that had transpired. Shortly afterwards, I went to bed feeling very exhausted.

I found myself at times wanting to fast from food so as to get serious about my pact with God. I would pray continually for Anna but especially when I was fasting. I would focus on my request and decided I would not give up until I got her back in my care. On the days when I chose to deny myself food, upon arriving at the office, my boss would bring in the most scrumptious bagels, pastries, breads, cheeses, fruits, and different types of meats for sandwiches. They were all so tempting. He would then ask me to help him with the preparation of the food for lunch for all of us in the office. I would do so at times without eating any of it, and he would keep saying "Miss Maria, aren't you going to eat?"

To which I would reply, "Not now, later."

I didn't want to broadcast what I was doing because I didn't want to draw attention to myself. This was a time between me and God.

When I would read my Bible, I would start recording some of the scriptures on index cards that were meaningful to my situation. I felt like these scriptures (see Appendix A) were written just for me. I would place them in the drawer next to my bed, and when I felt really discouraged I would pull them out and read them. I would remind the Lord of His promises to me through His Word. I would fall asleep sometimes reading them. I just believed that somehow He would see my circumstances and help me. After all, He was God and could do anything.

There was so much encouragement from my friends, but I remembered this particular one so well. A friend of mine, Mary, gave me a note in church a few months before going to Germany. On it she wrote, "Maria, you are only eight steps away from a miracle in Jesus' name." Mary."

A DREAM AND A PROPHECY

I started feeling a bit more optimistic. I believed that the Lord was refreshing my spirit and sustaining me. I just knew that He would come through for me. I had seen Him open blind eyes, unstop deaf ears, and cause the lame to walk, so there was no doubt in my mind that he would answer my prayers. My faith was beginning to be stirred again. I kept thinking about my dream and just couldn't give up. It was one of those dreams that I believed would come to pass as He showed me. The only question now was, when?

Could the difficulty I was going through set the very atmosphere for a miracle? Could it be that I was experiencing a miracle in the beginning stages? What I had come to realize was that if I was going to get a great miracle, the conditions would not only be difficult, but impossible. I had already been experiencing many difficult stages which could prove to be prerequisites for this miracle. Life, unfortunately, teaches us some hard lessons—some of the very things that cause us deep sorrows and much pain at times bring us the greatest joy. How ironic—a miracle seems to get birthed out of the most desperate or dire circumstances in life. Unfortunately, suffering, pain, sorrow, or even death, all seem to be strange requirements for some of the processes of life.

I decided to call my friend, Corine, in North Carolina and talk with her since she was always a source of encouragement to me. During the course of our conversation, she told me that she had had a vision from the Lord. In it, she described *seeing Anna at the age of about six years old. I was holding her hand, and we were walking, but it appeared as if we were in another country, and Paul was a few steps behind us.* She didn't know which country. She was convinced that I was going to get Anna back. I reminded her of the dream I had also of *Anna and me sitting on a bench together, and that I got her back.* She emphasized that the Lord was faithful and that He would bring it to pass. I was encouraged.

I received a call from her a few weeks later, and she was very excited to give me an 800 number to call that offered help with missing children. She happened to be listening to a radio program of a man being interviewed about his successes in returning many missing children. She insisted that I call the number and try to speak with someone at the organization. I figured it must have been worth a try, since Corine thought it was a good idea. Yet, I felt no motivation to call. So I wrote the number on a small piece of paper and tucked it in my billfold. I was so tired of all the negative responses I had received so far, that I had no interest in trying another number. I thought about this 800 number, and all I could feel was doubt. I thought about the fact that this was yet another number to call and probably another daunting process that would build my hopes up for another terrible fall.

Then I thought about all the attempts I had made to find my baby girl. Besides what seemed like hundreds of pleas to Paul to return her, I had already contacted more than eleven different sources for help, none of which were either willing or able to provide any assistance.

Those organizations were:

1. The National Center for Missing and Exploited Children—Wash. D.C.
2. Bureau of Missing Children—Perrine, Florida
3. U.S. Ambassador to Jamaica—Kingston, Jamaica

4. U.S. Consul/American Embassy—Kingston, Jamaica

5. FBI—Miami, Florida

6. Cooper City Police—Cooper City, FL

7. State Attorney's office—Ft. Lauderdale, FL

8. Adam Walsh Foundation—FL

9. Prime Minister of Jamaica

10. The State Department—Washington, D.C.

11. The German Embassy—Miami, FL

CHAPTER 8

ANGEL IN DISGUISE

It was an ordinary day at work, and I was sitting at the front desk in the office answering the phones and performing my regular duties. As usual, I had a small radio on in the background. It was now past lunch time and one of my favorite programs came on. It was Point of View, hosted by Marlin Maddox. I was listening on and off when I heard Marlin mentioned his special guest and the work he was doing. I started listening more carefully because of the subject matter. They were talking about kidnapped children and custody. Then I heard Marlin introduced his guest again as **Mark Miller** from the **American Association for Lost Children.** He directed a few questions to Mark about the children he had recovered for the custodial parents and how he did not charge a fee. My ears perked up, and I really began to pay close attention now. I thought of all the other organizations that had made their fees clear to me up front. Instead, he spoke about doing fundraisers to help parents and that this was a ministry. This organization, to my surprise, was a Christian one. To me, this was an unprecedented bit of good news. Then Marlin gave out an 800 number, and I wrote it down.

Suddenly, something occurred to me: Corine, the 800 number, my billfold. I rushed to my purse and emptied my billfold until I found the piece of paper I had tucked away. The 800 number was identical to the one I had just heard on Point of View! Tears came to my eyes, and I couldn't stop crying. I had to turn around at my desk and pretend that I was doing something work related behind me. I just kept wiping my eyes. By now, if someone came to my desk, they would see my red and puffy eyes. Then I thought, "Lord, is this my answer? Is this my help?" I wanted to call right away, but I also wanted to hear the rest of the program. So I listened until it ended.

As soon as the program ended, my fingers were dialing the number. Someone answered, and I asked to speak with Mark Miller. She informed me that he was not in at the moment, but she would give him my message that I had called. I asked her if he would really return my call. She said he would, and that he usually returns his calls. I briefly explained to her that I had a child who was kidnapped by my ex-husband and was taken to Germany. She assured me that Mark would call me back. I hung up the phone. The rest of that day was like a background in my mind. My hands worked, while my heart raced and my mind grew more expectant and hopeful by the second.

THE PHONE CALL

That night, I did not receive a call from Mark. By Friday, April 12th, 1991 at around 9:45 p.m., I heard the sound I had been desperately waiting for: the ring of the telephone. The voice on the line said, "This is Mark Miller, how can I help you?"

I introduced myself, and as I started telling him about Anna, I just choked up and began to cry. He immediately said to me, "Stop crying, we're gonna help you." Then he asked me if I had custody of my child, and I told him yes. He commented that that was very important since he worked only with those parents who had proof of custody. He also told me that he was going to send me a packet with some forms for me to fill out and return to him. He also mentioned that he wanted me to speak with a Donna, who lived relatively nearby in the West Palm Beach area. She had her two boys missing and was working on some fundraisers there for Mark's association. He thought that I might get some encouragement from her, and he wanted me to meet her. We spoke for about twenty-five minutes, and with each minute, my sense of hope simply multiplied.

Donna was truly a source of inspiration for me. After we spoke on the phone, I received a letter from her with scriptures of encouragement. Only two weeks after we met, Mark found her boys in Tennessee, and I was greatly encouraged.

The packet arrived from Mark, and I opened it in a hurry. A profile about the association was enclosed. The stories of the children who were returned to their custodial parents were phenomenal. I read them over and over in sheer amazement. My hope was being renewed. There were references to interviews of Mark on CNN's *Larry King Live, 48 hours, Hardcopy, Inside Edition,* and *Reader's Digest. Life* magazine also did a special on the incredible work he was doing for missing children. He was like an angel in disguise. In fact, on March 2nd, 1990, the Mayor of Houston declared a Mark Miller Day in his honor. Continental Airlines also flew him free of charge to recover the kids.

For the first time in this quest for Anna, I felt I was in good hands. His record was so impressive.

I completed my packet and sent it off to Mark. He called to confirm that he had received it, and everything looked good. He then asked me if AnnaMaria was listed in the national computer as a missing child. I told him she was not. He directed me immediately to the Police Department to register AnnaMaria. I made an appointment at the Cooper City Police Department, and an officer diligently entered AnnaMaria Rachael Silvera in the national database of missing children.

A few days after speaking with Mark, I decided to call the State Department to find out if any laws were passed that would help me get my child back from Germany. I was informed that a Child Abduction Act was signed under The Hague Convention in December of 1990. Unfortunately, my case which took place in 1986 was not retroactive. Needless to say, that was not encouraging news for me. The person I spoke with also offered to make a diplomatic visit on my behalf to see AnnaMaria in Germany and report back to me as to how she was doing. I realized immediately that what he had suggested would be nothing short of sabotaging our own mission, since it would only put Paul on notice. I thanked him for his offer but explained that I didn't think it was a very good idea in this situation. It was now clear to us that we would have to work swiftly, discretely, and without the support of the German authorities.

As I was pouring over all the logistics of physically traveling with Anna to leave Germany, her citizenship status presented itself in my mind. Although she was a United States citizen by birth, her father had obtained Jamaican citizenship as well. What was the chance that Anna was now also a German citizen? Suppose they chose not to grant her an exit from their country without a special visa? Without a legal adoption by Paul's German wife, Anna was unlikely to be a German citizen. This was now the window of opportunity I was going to take. It was a risk, but a necessary one. Only time would tell.

My next assignment from Mark was to obtain a passport for AnnaMaria. He confirmed what I had suspected, that we could neither enter nor leave Europe without one. The question now was how would we get a passport for her without a current photo? He then asked me if I had one. My reply was, sadly, "No." He suggested that I try to get one and then have a passport picture made from that photo. That was going to be a challenging task, but I would do anything to facilitate Mark's success.

A few days later, I was talking with my niece, Golda, and mentioned to her that I needed a recent picture of Anna. She informed me that her mother had received one from Paul. The problem was that her mother was a bit annoyed with me for not allowing Paul to see David. I did not appreciate her insensitivity towards my situation, especially since she was the one who sheltered me from Paul during the initial months after Anna's disappearance.

However, Golda said to me: "Maria, forget Mommy's attitude and go get the picture of your child. Swallow your pride and go because she won't let me have the picture to show you."

Well, she was right, and I needed to do just that.

I did swallow my pride and showed up at her house in Miami unannounced. She was taken by surprise but still invited me along with David to come in. I saw the framed 8x10 picture she had of Anna and John Paul (her brother through her father's marriage) on her upright piano. I asked her if I could make a copy of the picture and promised faithfully to return the original to her. She hesitated at first, but I gave her my word that I would return it. She agreed and allowed me to take the picture to copy it. We visited for awhile, and then we left.

I stared at my daughter for what seemed like an eternity. She was smiling the same big, bright smile that I remembered so vividly. Her face was bigger now but maintained all the same beautiful features. There she was, posing with the only little brother she knew at that time. She and her *first* little brother deserved to have a picture just like that together. As I reveled in the photograph, imagining it come alive with speech and laughter and "I love you," I also felt the piercing pain that she was still so far out of reach. "That is about to change, little Anna," I thought. "I am coming to get my baby girl."

The problem with the picture was that John Paul's shoulder was blocking Anna's cheek and left shoulder. I got a copy made however and returned the original, as promised. I then called Mark and told him that I had completed my assignment, but that Anna's shoulder was being blocked in the photo. He said that that should not pose a problem because some photography shops had artists who could correct the problem easily. I found such a photographer and explained what I wanted done, and sure enough, after the artwork was completed the picture was reduced, and we got a perfect passport picture.

My blood was now flowing with excitement and anticipation. With no time to delay, I quickly applied for her American passport. I had an original copy of her birth certificate, and I, as her mother, could legitimately sign the form for her passport. That was permitted since she was a minor. I paid the fee and off went the forms. I was told it would take anywhere from six to eight weeks before I would receive the passport. I started praying that I would receive it soon without any hitches or delays. The funny thing was, during this time, I had a dream, and in it, I dreamt *that I was buying a blow-drying brush and was telling someone in the store that I was going to Germany.*

Time kept passing by, and there was no sign of the passport. It was now about six weeks since I had applied for it. I kept praying, "Lord, where is the passport?" Then one night, I had a dream that *I received the passport in the mail.* I said to David, "We're going to get the passport soon!"

He said, "Yep" as if he knew for sure that we would get it soon. He was so cute and agreeable.

It was on Saturday, June 29th, 1991, about two weeks after the dream, when I went to check my mailbox. There was the envelope I was waiting and praying for all these nights. I recognized it and quickly took it out of the mailbox and ran in the house and shouted, "Da, Da, we got the passport!" and I jumped so high with excitement in the kitchen that my head touched the panels on the ceiling. This was the major breakthrough I needed. What seemed so impossible was now a reality! In a way, Anna's passport was now my passport to get my child back.

Immediately, my fingers started dialing the number to Mark's office. I told him I got the passport, and he was very pleased to hear the news. He immediately gave me my next task, to start making plans to go to Germany. He inquired about contact information for Paul. I told him I had received a post office box number in an attempt to try and communicate with my child. Mark Miller used this number and was able to obtain a physical address for Paul in Germany. Each week we were making more progress. I was continually amazed at Mark's ingenuity and skills; he was truly gifted in his field.

Mark received a call shortly after the radio program was aired from a retired member of the C.I.A. He happened to be listening to the same program that connected me to the American Association for Lost Children. He had recently become a Christian and was very moved by the work Mark was doing. He was calling in to volunteer his services. Mark told him that he was about to conduct his first international case and offered for him to go with us to Germany. He emphatically agreed to go. Continental Airlines showed their support to the American Association for Lost Children by assisting with flight passes for the volunteers. That was such a blessing.

All this time, the prayer group that I had been a part of was continually praying with me for Anna's return. Some of the members at the church I attended were also praying for her. I had friends in different places praying that we would be united one day.

By now, you can see that I have very interesting dreams. In this one, I dreamt that *AnnaMaria came to our apartment at Pine Island Ridge. She appeared to be very happy and was playing with David.*

I WOULD SEARCH THE WORLD

Around the first week in July of 1991, I received a letter from my daughter, Malaika, with a poem included that she wrote about Anna. Even to this day, whenever I read this poem, it brings tears to my eyes.

> *Long Lost Sister*
> *Six years ago*
> *You came into my world*
> *There you were*
> *A precious baby girl*
> *Little did you know*
> *Of the story*
> *That would soon unfurl*

Five years ago
You were taken away...
I cannot forget
How much I cried that day
Innocent and pure,
How were you to know
The pain our mother
Was to endure?

Four years ago
I made to you a vow
That I would search the world
As long as time allows
To bring Mama her little girl
...For her heart was hurting now...

Three years ago
You were still not home
There was our Mama
With her only son alone
It felt as if you were gone forever
It felt as if you'd never come home

Two years ago
Mama had a dream
You had returned
And life was normal, it seemed
But a dream is not reality

For reality is never a dream
And when our Mama awoke
Her little girl had not returned

One year ago
We got word that you were ill,
The pain of such knowledge
Made the yearning greater still
There was nothing Mama could do
To ease your pain and take care of you

I hope you are doing well
But only time will tell
Little sister, I'm singing this song
Because I hope it won't be long
I trust that very soon
I'll hold you in my arms
and say:
"Welcome home, my sweet
AnnaMaria Rachael

Malaika

This poem has meant a lot to me. I remember reading it many times, and each time, I would sit and cry just reflecting on how prophetic it was. She was describing the circumstances so well and ending on a note that everyone wanted to see become reality. It brought me so much consolation, but more importantly, it showed me clearly how much Malaika loved Anna and cared enough about her to want to search the world for her, and I knew she would. She was truly my angel trying to encourage me and bring me hope.

I remember driving to work one morning while listening to the radio, and Zig Zigler made this resounding statement: "Tough times never last, only tough people do." That statement has remained with me as a reminder to be tough and not let my circumstances pull me down; that I need to really fight and give it my best shot; that I should not give in to barriers, frustration, fear and depression. I must prevail in these circumstances; I must be victorious.

I realize now that I could not afford for my spirit to be downcast. I had to fight depression and all its offshoots. The struggle had begun. I was still battling with bad migraines and neck pains. My job was extremely demanding with heavy telephone contacts. I was barely coping with the load of taking care of David, working fulltime, and staying on track with the rest of our busy lives. I was unable to get enough rest. I awakened nightly and had tremendous difficulty going back to sleep. I was in a perpetual state of exhaustion. It was too much for one person to handle. I would pray and ask the Lord to help me. He sustained me and kept me. His Word was life giving and encouraging to me. I realized that I had to continue exercising my faith in all things. I had to endure.

During this time, I also had to continue practicing forgiveness which was very hard given my circumstances. I learned later that a comment was made by someone in a group of friends and acquaintances of mine. The comment was: "How is she going to take care of another child?" That person basically thought it was a crazy idea for me to go after my child since I was struggling financially. That was easy for that person to say, as he tucked his children safely into bed each night. The real question was: How would he react if one of his kids was missing? Where was the faith we were taught to have as Christians? Where was the love we were to have one for another? Should money be the determining factor of whether a mother should raise her daughter? Yes, it's necessary, but should it determine the premium or value we place on life? Could a mother forget the child she bore?

THANKSGIVING AND PRAISE

I started reflecting on how God wanted me to function and live before Him. I knew that the Bible taught principles that encouraged me to practice faith because this, it described, is the only way in which I could please Him. In other words, to have faith operating in my life, I must believe that I had received the thing before I got it. That is the basis of faith. Moreover, I knew I needed to start having an attitude of thanksgiving before I got what I wanted (the reverse of what we are taught in society). So, I had to believe that I got AnnaMaria back before I did. More importantly, God expected me to believe that He is; that He is capable of answering my prayers. Most of us have a very detached concept of who God is. He wants us to come to Him as a child would to a natural father. He wants us to trust Him with confidence and not doubt. Most times we don't get our prayers answered because we don't believe they will be answered. My situation was too difficult for me to handle; I needed supernatural intervention. This difficulty I encountered would ultimately create the very atmosphere for a miracle. My situation was not only difficult, but impossible which would set the stage for a great miracle. The way I latched on to God like a child clinging to the hand of a parent made my desperate situation a delight to Him.

The ingredients of praise and thanksgiving are so important because these are what pleases the heart of God more than anything else. I kept thinking of the reference in the Psalms about how God resists the proud but gives grace to the humble. Would I let pride hold me back at this juncture? The Lord is pleased with a thankful, grateful heart and rewards such ones. Praise, I believe is the most vital part before a miracle occurs.

THE VICTORY DANCE

I remember one Sunday afternoon, I was lying down just resting before going to the evening service. These thoughts kept going through my head that I should praise the Lord in the dance as David did in the Bible with all his might, before all the people. I felt in my heart that the Holy Spirit was whispering to me that He would bless me for my obedience if I did; but I was so scared.

For me, this seemed an impossible task to go and dance before all those people, even though I loved to dance before the Lord and just worship Him in private. I was just nervous about going out in front of such a large crowd. Both young and old, at times, would express their praise and worship corporately unto the Lord in the dance and in songs with instruments as described in the Psalms. At various times, solo pieces would also be done by some of the more experienced dancers.

So the time came, and we went to church. Close to the end of the praise and worship part of the service, Pastor Buck got up and said, "I really believe there is someone here tonight that should praise the Lord in the dance."

I immediately knew in my heart that he was referring to me because of the desire I had to worship the Lord in the dance. I became so nervous and turned to my girlfriend who was sitting next to me and said, "Gloria, he is speaking to me."

She turned to me and said, "So what are you waiting for?" and then she stepped out in the aisle to make way for me to get out.

By then, I was really shaking. Yet, suddenly, my mind reflected on the fact that this was the God of all creation I was about to praise. He had designed the process of life and created all things, including me, and why should I not praise Him with everything that was within me? After all, He gave me life. So, why should I care or worry about what people should think? So what if I made a fool of myself? Besides, He was the only one who could help me now, only He could move upon my circumstances and change them for me. He was the only one who could answer my prayers. I would now praise Him above all things and circumstances.

I proceeded forth with a new momentum and drive. The King of Kings, I thought, was on my side. His spirit was with me. He was the one motivating me, and no one could stop me now. I was wearing a white on white embroidered skirt and a white shirt. I made one step, then two, and before I could realize it, my arms were up in the air, and my feet were following. I remembered turning and moving slowly across the area in front of the platform. My eyes were mostly closed just opening briefly to make my next turn. I felt as if I was elevated about ten inches off the ground. I had entered the heavenly realm, as it were. I almost forgot I was still on the earth. I was worshipping my Maker, and I had completed my Victory Dance like the song of victory sung in ancient days before the battle was fought. Now I could rest knowing the battle truly belonged to the Lord because He promised that He would fight for us. I had now put it in His hands. He was perfectly capable.

I made it back to my seat, and when I looked around, I could see people wiping their eyes and praising the Lord even more. It was a really special time in the presence of the Lord. I was so blessed and refreshed. I had achieved the impossible as far as I was concerned. I believed I moved the Hand of God. I also believed He took note of me even more that evening. I knew He was pleased with my sacrifice of

117

worship because I delighted in Him. I had read in the Psalms that if we delight ourselves in the Lord, He would give us the desires of our hearts. He knew how hard it was for me to transcend the fear of man, but I did. I believe I experienced tid bits of what King David experienced when he danced before the Lord. He didn't care who was watching or who approved. He just wanted to worship the King of Kings from the depths of his being to offer his thanksgiving. God knew I offered up a true sacrifice of praise to Him. He knew my frame and what I was made of. It was like a sweet-smelling savor unto Him. He was well pleased.

CHAPTER 9

PREPARING FOR
THE GREAT JOURNEY

The days seemed to gallop by very quickly. I found myself frequently speaking with Mark Miller on the phone or leaving messages for him with one of the volunteers at the organization regarding our plans for Germany. Mark had decided that we should try to leave sometime around the first part of November.

I started my own fund-raising activities for Mark's organization, while still attempting to remain discrete about my plans to go to Germany. I sent a letter to most of my friends, seeking donations for the AALC. The response was positive and generous. This is a sample of the letter I wrote and sent out on May 17th, 1991:

Dear Val:

The purpose of my writing to you at this time is to brief you concerning AnnaMaria, my daughter, that my ex-husband abducted nearly 5 years ago. He took her from me at 10 ½ months old under the pretense of taking her to the beach, and then took off with her to Jamaica. He threatened my life concerning her and said she would never return to the United States.

Well, I refused to accept that, and even though, when he took her, neither of us had custody, I have been awarded full custody since then. I was commissioned by the Judge to take her in my care at once. Unfortunately, that has not happened yet due to the fact that I was not given the assistance needed to perform such a task. I contacted numerous organizations for help, but none came to my aid.

I sort of gave up hope of ever getting her back, but somehow, the reality of the injustice that had happened dawned on me. This made me realize that life is unfair, and more frighteningly, that it almost appears as if the law is not designed to protect the innocent but rather the guilty.

In my desperation for help, I appealed to the police, different bureaus for missing children, including the Bureau for Missing and Exploited Children in Washington D.C., the FBI, the United States ambassador to Jamaica, the U.S. consul in Jamaica, the state attorney's office in Florida, the German consulate, and finally, the State Department.

You must understand that when the abduction occurred there was no law in the U.S. to protect American citizens that were removed from the boundaries of the court. Finally, in December of 1990, the Child Abduction Act was signed which now protects U.S. citizens internationally. Unfortunately, I was told by the State Department that my case was not retroactive. In other words, I cannot get any help with AnnaMaria since she was taken in 1986. They offered however, to make an official visit from the State Department to see her and report to me as to how she was doing. I refused such a mission simply because that would just put Paul on notice as to my attempts to get her back.

So, even though all the doors were slammed shut in my face, I decided to fight for my child whose rightful place is with me. I believe that where there is life, there is hope. I believe the Creator of all mankind is capable of ruling the *hearts of all men and surely render JUSTICE in this situation.*

I have finally found an organization that cares and is willing to help me get her back. So, I am trying to get donations from as many sources as I can. These donations are tax deductible. Also, some literature about them is enclosed for you to see some of the wonderful things they have done.

Any amount will be greatly appreciated. Please note on your donation to the American Association for Lost Children that it's for AnnaMaria Silvera. I do appreciate anything you can do for all abducted children.

Thank You,

Maria Nicholas

We also collected donations outside the Publix Supermarket near our apartment. Thanks to some of our friends, including Amy and Kelly who helped us.

I called the State Department again on October 11th, 1991 shortly before I left for Germany in an effort to find out if there were any international laws governing me taking my child. He informed me that I should be able to leave Germany without a problem. However, he added that if Paul had obtained custody of AnnaMaria through the German courts I could in fact be held and jailed there if he notified the authorities. That, of course, did not sound very comforting to me. I realized that I was now on my own and had to accept this most feared risk. I thought about my daughter, and that I might risk being separated from all my children if I was arrested in Germany. Faith, however, consoled my fears. I knew Anna belonged with me, and there had to be a way to get her out of Germany safely. My missing daughter was certainly worth the risk.

I called the German Consulate in Miami to see what information or help I could obtain. I was told there was nothing they could do to help me.

Up to this point, one part of me had no hesitation about going to Germany, yet the other part was encountering doubts and fear. Each day presented another circumstance that caused me to wonder "What if?" Stress was rearing its ugly head in various forms. I was fighting severe migraines with painkillers throughout these days. Sleep at night was no longer a guarantee. Concentration by day was becoming more of a struggle. It was so difficult to function and plan for this trip, but I was determined not to give up. If I died in the process, then so be it. I would have died fighting for what was rightfully mine.

I also discussed our plans with my friends, Carol and Rusty. Without saying much, Rusty decided to ask some of his co-workers if they would donate frequent flyer miles for my ticket to Germany. He got enough miles for our tickets, but frequent flyer miles could not be used for Anna's ticket since it would originate in Germany. I would have to purchase a ticket for her.

One Sunday at church, my pastor asked how things were going, and I mentioned I needed a ticket for Anna, and I was praying that the Lord would provide the finances. He said, "Don't worry the church will help with her ticket." I later found out that an anonymous gift of $750 had been left for me at the church to help with my trip. I believed my dear friends Carol and Rusty had donated the money. Later, in a conversation, Carol hesitatingly admitted, when I asked, that they did. They are such gracious people.

Things started falling into place little by little. I now had Anna's passport, tickets, and extra cash in hand to pay hotel expenses. Now I needed some gifts to take for Anna.

I wanted to take her a doll, a coat, an outfit, a pair of shoes, a purse, some hair clips, a comb, brush, and a mirror. I thought most little girls her age would love to play with such things. I also decided to take the doll she left with me as a connecting point between us and a few family pictures (including her father and grandparents). In fact, I thought the pictures might work to my advantage on a number of levels, reconnecting any cloudy memories she might have of her time with me in Florida. The only thing I had difficulty with was picking out a dress and a pair of shoes for her. I didn't know how big or small she was, so I just had to take a chance. It turned out I wasn't too far off.

Roughly two weeks before our departure, I had another dream: *I was on the plane headed to Germany. When I arrived, I picked up Anna and simply made a turnaround and was headed back to Miami safely.*

I had yet another dream a few days before leaving for Germany: *I was talking with Paul in Germany.* I thought about my dream the next morning and said, "I don't want to see him. I hope I don't see him."

One day, at prayer group just before leaving for Germany, on Wednesday, October 16th, 1991, Gary encouraged me about getting AnnaMaria back. He read this scripture to me from Isaiah 49:25*: "Surely, says the Lord, even the captives of the mighty will be taken away and the prey of the tyrant will be rescued; for I will contend with the one who contends with you and I will save your children."*

THE DEPARTURE

The date was set for us to leave for Germany. Mark, along with two volunteers, made arrangements to leave from Houston, Texas, and I left from Miami, Florida. We planned to meet at the international baggage area of the airport in Frankfurt.

My friend Lily offered to keep David for me until I returned from Germany. She gave me a ride to the airport early that morning. Before we said goodbye, I hugged David and whispered in his ears that I was going to get Anna. He smiled and gave me a big hug. It was so hard to leave him; I missed him so much.

I checked in with American Airlines and about an hour and a half later, I boarded American flight 523 which departed at 7:45 a.m. on Tuesday, the 5th of November 1991 for Dallas, Texas. I prayed before we took off for a safe flight.

Once we were airborne, my mind started racing. I kept wondering how we were going to get Anna. I kept reflecting on the various strategies used by Mark Miller's teams in previous rescue missions. Which approach would we use for my little girl? Would we try to follow her to school or watch for opportunities in order to snatch her? The truth was, no one had formulated a plan yet. All that was obtained was an address for Paul. We would have to develop our plan when we reached Germany. As the mother in this case, there was no question about my willingness to embark upon this dangerous adventure. The remarkable thing was there were three others willing to take that risk with me in order to reunite us. Each time I thought of these three "soldiers" who were on their way to fight for and with me, I could hardly comprehend it. Clearly, there were still good people left in this world. I assured myself that it was going to be fine and that the Lord was our Helper.

The plane touched down in Dallas at around 9:50 a.m. I had a layover of about four hours and forty-five minutes. I used that time to call Mark's office to see if there was a message for me. I was informed that my party of three had already departed for Frankfurt. We were literally on our way. I was actually making the trip to find my daughter!

I decided to call and let my mother know that I was headed to Germany to try and get Anna. She was struck by surprise to learn of this latest development. She gave stern caution to be careful. I asked her not to mention it to anyone. I just could not afford for this information to reach the Silvera family, not now, not when we were so close.

I also called my older daughter, Malaika, at the University of Wisconsin. I had promised to keep her updated at each location. I told her I was headed to Frankfurt. She was happy that the time had finally come to get Anna back, but the worry in her voice was inescapable. She knew the type of person Paul was and the unpredictability of his personality. She knew how skilled he was with a gun. She also experienced his awful temper and repeated threats when she lived with us. She was now worried that I might get hurt or even killed. She kept telling me to be careful. With all my assurances and promises, I just knew she would be worried. She informed me that she would not attend any classes that week, but instead she would sit by the telephone around the clock. She would wait for my every call, especially after we made it to Germany. We prayed before saying goodbye.

We finally took off from Dallas on American Airlines Flight 70 at 2:45 p.m. and arrived in Frankfurt at 7:30 a.m. I was exhausted from sleep deprivation. I always have difficulty sleeping on airplanes, so I managed to get a bit of reading done and reviewed my pocket dictionary of German/English expressions. I located some key phrases that would be necessary on our mission.

SPIES IN THE LAND

I had now set foot on the enemy's territory. What would it be like in this totally foreign culture? Would I run into Paul as my dreams were indicating? Would there be delays and obstacles? Would we get lost? Would we eventually get to this address and find that they no longer lived there?

Would Paul try to hurt me or my group, or worse yet, Anna? Would Anna be on that returning flight? Time would tell.

In the meantime, I had about a five-hour wait before my team arrived. I stood in the same location for about an hour and a half. I could not sit in the restaurant close by because of the cigarette smoke. It seemed like everyone in there was smoking, and I have difficulty breathing whenever I am around smoke. I watched people come and go, and I was getting a little weary. Finally, a young African-American soldier who was checking in the arriving military personnel for duty in Germany noticed me. He wanted to know why I was standing there so long and suggested that I go inside and rest my feet. I explained my smoke allergy, and we ended up talking for a little while. He was very pleasant, and he seemed genuine and caring. It was comforting to make a friend in such a strange, large place. When the five hours had finally passed, I bid him farewell and headed for international baggage claims.

I waited there for another hour. The anticipation and anxiety was building again. Finally, the guys arrived on Continental Flight 50 at 12:30 p.m. I identified Mark from the American Association for Lost Children by the T-shirt he was wearing. He towered over the others with his height of 6'7", and he weighed about 245 pounds. The retired member of the C.I.A weighed about 250 pounds and was about 6'1" tall. The smallest member of the group was about 5'6" and weighed roughly 145 pounds. This was the profile of our rescue crew.

They got their bags, and we took a taxi to a car rental facility. Before we drove off from the airport, we noticed a multitude of Mercedes Benz cars that were being used as taxi cabs. It just seemed so unusual since those cars are considered luxury cars in the United States. They were in striking abundance there.

After a couple of hours at the car rental facility, we were finally issued a vehicle. We then set out to find a restaurant since we were all very hungry. After we were seated in the restaurant, I reached for my pocket language "help book." Our waiter spoke very little English so there was my opportunity to recite some of the German sentences I had familiarized myself with. The guys thought I was a genius since we were able to order our meals. We all had a good laugh including the waiter. He thought my German was "good," and I was proud of my small linguistic accomplishment.

By this time, I had had no sleep since I left Miami. I was so sleepy that I was ready to collapse anywhere. My eyes were almost sticking together from lack of sleep. The guys had all slept on the plane so they were going along without much problem. I was the one hurting now from sleep deprivation; headaches and neck pains were now being manifested.

After we left the restaurant, we went looking for a hotel to spend the night. We located one but didn't check in until later that evening. Mark wanted to drive to Wiesbaden to see if he could find an address for a young African-American girl who was abducted by her father and was living there with his girlfriend. She was about eight years old, and Mark's desire was to try and help the girl's mother locate her. Since we were going to be in Germany, he wanted to attempt to do both cases, if possible.

We drove to Wiesbaden and found the address of the apartment complex. We could not get inside because of a guard who was seated at the front entrance. We sat in the car hoping and praying that the little girl would come outside to play. Mark and Buddy decided to walk towards the back of the building in hopes of finding her while the other volunteer and I waited in the car. I had just looked at the girl's picture in her file and within a few minutes later, she came walking out the front entrance of the building. I quickly opened the car door, got out of my seat, and started walking in her direction. I intended to engage her in some form of conversation so as to delay her for Mark and Buddy to be able to see her. Well, it worked. I said hello to her and asked her if she spoke English, and she told me she did. Then I asked her if she knew of a supermarket close by. She said she didn't know of one. By then, Mark and Buddy started appearing up the sidewalk towards us. They said hi to her and realized without saying anything else that she was the girl they were trying to find. We simply said goodbye to her and went into the car and drove off. Our mission was accomplished. Mark had gained the information he wanted. She was in that building, but we could not take her, only her mother could. That was the law, as enforced by Mark Miller in every case. He did not touch any child but directed the custodial parents to claim them.

We searched for a pay phone. Once we found one, Mark called the girl's mother in Texas and reported that he had seen her daughter and that she should arrange travel to Germany as soon as possible. She assured Mark that she would be on the next available flight out of Houston.

She made arrangements for both her and her sister to travel that same day. They arrived in Frankfurt the next morning, and we picked them up at the airport, got them some sandwiches, and dropped them off at the hotel where we were staying.

We were now *en route* to Bielefeld to get Anna. We had a late start because we had detoured via the airport in Frankfurt in order to get Claudette and her sister. We eventually arrived in Bielefeld after nightfall.

On our way there, we were all praying that God would give us wisdom as to what we should do. We had no idea what would transpire. We started off on the Autobahn by playing one of my Hosanna music cassettes. I was prepared for everything. My music was my consolation and very important for my mental well-being. It soothed my nerves and calmed me down and helped to put my mind at ease.

We drove by landscapes that were picturesque. They were simply very beautiful. The mountains were majestic, and the entire countryside seemed so manicured. Everything was so well maintained. It was kind of strange seeing all the signs written in German along the way. It registered then that we were in a different country. The culture was so different, but we were enjoying the ride and the beautiful architecture along the way. It wasn't long though before it got dark, and we were trying to figure out our way to Bielefeld.

After driving for over an hour, we started discussing a possible approach to use after our arrival in North Germany. We decided that Mark should introduce himself once we were at Silvera's door. Then I suggested that one of our team members should act as if he were on an official visit from the U.S.A. being a former member of the C.I.A. We were convinced that he could cultivate that look. This would be an attempt to try and intimidate Paul a bit. We had a clipboard in the car so I suggested again that we put a copy of my custody order on it and have him hold it in his hand and also wear Mark's Honorary Deputy Sheriff's badge that was given to him by the State of Texas. We were busily devising a plan. I interjected that no one should let Paul out of sight because he was known for the unpredictable.

We prayed again and asked the Lord to help us find Paul's address by directing us to the location. I prayed that He would protect us and that He would show us favor and allow us to get AnnaMaria. As we finished praying, we started listening to the music again. We were all singing or humming along with the tape. We had picked up a momentum now and felt we could pursue the battle. We had gained strength.

ON ENEMY'S TURF

We arrived in Bielefeld at around 8:00 p.m. It took us close to five hours to get there. We kept driving around in circles trying to find the street address to Paul's apartment. As we circled one more time, trying to locate the street sign, I saw a taxi-cab parked on the side of the road with the driver just sitting inside. I knew cab drivers were very familiar with addresses and that he would more than likely be able to help us find the address.

I said to Mark, "If there is anyone who knows a city, it would be a cab or bus driver. The Lord has that cab driver waiting there to show us where to go, let's pay him, and let him direct us there."

Well, Mark took my suggestion and we paid him, and he led us to the street we were trying to find.

It so happened that we had driven up and down that street a few times before but we could not see the street sign because it was hidden by a tree limb and also because it was already dark.

We finally located the address, and it was not a gated community, so we parked the car outside the building for a little while. Mark then decided to try and find a pay phone in order to call the Silveras to see if they were at home.

We found a pay phone a few streets away from the apartment complex. Mark called the number, and Paul's wife answered the phone. He quickly muttered some sort of gibberish that could not be understood. She then passed the phone to Paul, who said, "Hello." Mark then hung up the phone after confirming that they were indeed at home.

We drove back to the apartment and sat in the car for a few more minutes. The first thing we did was to pray again and ask God to help us. We were all very nervous and did not know what to expect. I suggested that the car keys should be left under the mat on the driver's side and the car left unlocked. My reason for saying this was so that everyone would be able to get back in the car without it being locked. Also, we would not have to try and figure out who had the car keys. I also emphasized that they should not let Paul out of their sight at anytime because he could pull an element of surprise. They embraced that caution very well.

Our plan was for one of our men to knock on the door and ask to use the phone. After permission was granted, Mark would introduce himself. If there was any resistance, he intended to use his foot to block the door from being shut. He also instructed that I should not be with them when they arrived at the door but that I should be under the stairwell with Anna's coat over my head until they gave me my cue to come to the door. Imagine the danger of this scenario. We would have to stage an authorized seizure of an abducted child. There would be no German authorization, escort, or protection.

We prayed once more and then decided to enter the building. We walked up the stairs at first to the third floor trying to find the apartment, but the numbers were not written on the outside of the doors. We heard the voices of children in one of the apartments upstairs, but we did not knock. We bowed our heads right there and asked God to lead us to the right apartment. Mark then said, "Let's go back to the first floor." I took my place under the stairwell, and Mark knocked on the first apartment closest to the stairs. A few moments later, Paul's wife came to the door.

"Good evening, I wondered if you would be so kind to let me use your phone," Mark said in a pleasant voice. By that time, Paul emerged at the door to see who had knocked. Mark changed his tone abruptly. I could hear the conversation clearly from where I was.

"I'm Mark Miller from the American Association for Lost Children. Are you Mr. Silvera?"

I could hear Paul's faint acknowledgment with much trepidation from my hiding place. Mark then established that there was a child there by the name of AnnaMaria Rachael Silvera who was abducted by him from his former wife, Maria Nicholas. Next, our volunteer—former C.I.A. member—introduced himself, holding his clipboard with the custody papers for Paul to see.

"There is one more person with us," Mark said, as he motioned for me to join them.

I hurried to the doorway and looked Paul straight in the eye.

"Maria, what is this?" he growled. His eyes pierced mine with a seething rage.

"Where is she?" I demanded. He pointed to a back room. "She is sleeping," he insisted, but I had no intentions of keeping up a conversation with him.

I was on a mission to get my daughter. He was posturing himself as though he wanted to guard her from me. I looked at Mark, with a panicked expression. "Mark, do something!" I wanted to get my child and get out of there fast. To recall my dream before going to Germany, now I stood in front of Paul, face to face.

Mark pointed me towards the bedroom, "Maria, go in there and take your child!"

He could not do it, only I could; now was the moment I was waiting for all these years, now was the time to act as fast as my hands and legs could move. This was my grand opportunity to retrieve my child that was unfairly taken away from me. Fear mingled with hope paraded across my mind in flashes. I was struck as it were with instant panic but I kept going. I convinced myself in an instant that I couldn't fall apart now. I had to be strong even though I felt so weak. I had to do it. I had to get her. That was my goal.

But what if I got hurt in the process trying to get her out of her bed where she was sleeping?

"That's not fair," I heard his wife protesting, as I made my way to the back bedroom.

I thought to myself, *What's not fair? She's my child!* I immediately started towards the room, with my heart pounding and my body shaking like a leaf, in order to get Anna, when I heard Paul saying, "I have my custody papers in the room. Let me get them."

Then I heard Mark saying, "Don't move, we don't need to see them."

IN A FEW QUICK SECONDS

I reached Anna's bedroom in a matter of seconds and scooped her up from the bottom bunk bed where she was still asleep. My heart thumped so loudly that I thought surely everyone in the house could also hear it. My chest began to tighten as my head pounded that I thought I was going to collapse. I tried to take a deep breath but there was no time. My legs felt so weak they appeared as if they could hardly hold me up. I was so nervous I thought I would drop her when I picked her up from her bed. The adrenaline my body had manufactured in a hurry was now carrying me. I somehow mustered up the courage and managed to throw her over my shoulder and put the coat I had over her head. I didn't want her traumatized by the drama unfolding around her.

I came bolting out of the room towards the front door as I held my daughter close.

"No you can't take her," Paul shrieked as he lunged towards me.

Mark and one of the guys had him blocked in, and Paul wasn't strong enough to struggle with both of them. I made it through the door and down to the car. One of the guys followed close behind me with Mark only steps behind. We quickly got into the car with Mark in the driver's seat anticipating Buddy's entrance into the car.

Buddy was still in the apartment until we were safely in the car. "Get down and face the wall, man. I don't want to have to shoot you!" he ordered in his toughest voice.

He was only 5'6" and weighed only 145 pounds but was very convincing. He held his right hand under his t-shirt and made it appear as if it were a gun. Paul dropped to his knees and turned to the wall shaking. His wife just stood there wide-eyed.

"Don't you dare move," Buddy warned as he ran through the door and jumped in the car.

We sped off with our "prize" towards the Autobahn. The rescue had taken less than two minutes.

Anna was curled up beside me under her coat on the back seat of the car as Buddy caught his breath and replayed his final moments with Paul to us. The other guys were in the front watching for anyone who might have followed our car. We were cruising along with the flow of traffic on this European freeway, but we felt like we were moving at the speed of light. It was a feeling that could not be explained. We felt for sure no one could catch up with us. We were gone in a flash.

We were all experiencing different moods of excitement and exuberance. My mood for instance was one of shock. My heart was still racing, and my head continued pounding. My hands were also still shaking, and my blood vessels were operating on overtime. I could almost hear the thumps and thuds going on simultaneously between my heart and head. They were playing their own concertos of this great celebration.

I was still in awe of the fact that I had actually flown to a foreign country and retrieved my daughter. Where did I get such courage? Would Paul's threat to me become a reality now? It was all very hard to assimilate mentally at the moment. I realized however that when there is a will to do something, a way would always be provided. I was now experiencing that way; I had my child with me and no power on this earth was going to take her away from me. She belonged to me. It immediately dawned on me that I had overcome that awful thing called fear which intimidated me for so long with the thought of not being able to see my child again. It was now made very clear to me that because of my persistence and confidence in God, I was now enjoying the fruits of my labor. God truly was my helper, my confidence, my high tower and my strength.

She was still sleeping beside me, as I sat frozen in my seat. It all seemed so unreal I just didn't know what to do or say. Should I wake her up, or would I have to wait for her to awaken by herself? Would she resemble the picture I saw of her in my dream? Her size appeared to be what I saw, but what about her face? Would it look identical to the one I saw in my dream or would I be disappointed? I was overcome with curiosity. I wanted to see what she looked like so much; I could hardly wait.

THE UMBILICAL CONNECTION

I could not wait a minute longer. I decided to carefully lift the coat to peek at her face, only to realize that she was already awake, with a few teardrops on her cheek.

"Hi darling, I'm your mommy," I said softly, stroking her beautiful curly hair.

"No, my mommy is at home with John Paul," she replied.

"No darling, I'm the mommy who had you in her tummy," I explained, pointing to my stomach.

She seemed confused since she had only known the German woman to be her mother. She knew nothing about me. She was never told that I was her mother. In fact, I was a total stranger to her. It hurt so much that words are inadequate to explain what transpired at that moment. I was instantly faced with a genuine form of rejection from my own child and only love could absorb it and help me not to judge her for her ignorance. I braced myself and thought that love does not receive a hurt. There was nothing in my mind that she could say or do to me at this point that could cause me not to love her. She had been told lies by her father, and I had to change that picture for her. I instantly had to draw on all my resources to assist me in helping her understand and hope she would accept this frightening truth. After all, she was now only six years old and too young to fully understand all that had happened. Besides, this was the first time I was seeing her for the past five years and four months.

I had her in my arms now, and no power on this earth could change that. I was going to succeed with her.

"Lord, please give me the right words to say to her," I prayed quietly, and He most certainly did. I then drew her towards me and gave her a kiss on her cheek and said, "I love you very much." She just kept quiet, looking down at her hands. "Look at what I brought you," I immediately said, in an attempt to break the ice, so to speak. Right then, I reached over and got the bag with the things I had brought her. I pulled out a new doll first, then a small blue purse with all sorts of clips, a mirror and a comb and brush. She was immediately lost in it all. I then reached for the baby doll she had left behind with me. As I handed it to her, I had to restrain my emotions when I said, "This is your baby doll that you left with me."

She took it from me and looked at it but was more interested in the new one. The one she left behind had all the evidences of how toddlers treat dolls. Soil marks were obvious which served as such reminders to me of how she used to embrace it and drag it all over the house. If only she knew that she wouldn't go to sleep without it most times. Poor dollie! She just couldn't identify with her at the moment; there were memory problems.

"If you lost your baby doll, would you go looking for her?" I asked her. She emphatically said, "Yah!" I then interjected that that's what I had done. I told her that I had lost my baby doll and that I went looking for her, and now I found her." She looked at me a bit puzzled but didn't say anything, so I smiled at her. This was my golden opportunity to explain to her what had happened.

"You see, your daddy asked me if he could take you to the beach, and I agreed, but he never brought you back, and he said if I tried to get you back he would kill me."

She immediately exclaimed in her cute German accent, "Oh, oh, that's not good. I'm going to tell Nellie [her friend] that daddy wanted to dead you."

Those were her exact words. In her mind that's how she understood it. I realized then that the words had slipped right out of my mouth. I thought they appeared a bit strong, yet I wanted her to know the truth without it being diluted. To my surprise, she handled it extremely well. She appeared to be so mature, well-adjusted, and intelligent for her age. It was obvious to me that she was well taken care of with no apparent signs of abuse.

LOST YEARS RESTORED

I then reached for a mini-album I had also brought with me. In it, I had put a few of her dedication pictures seen with her dad and me, his mother and father, who are her grandma and grandpa. Also included was a picture of David, her brother, who was not yet born when she was taken. When she saw it she exclaimed, "I have one like that in my room, he's my brother, and he lives in America."

It was apparent that the copy of David's picture I had sent to her grandparents in Jamaica was sent to Germany, and she had it in her room. That was a plus for me. It worked on a number of levels to connect us. She became very interested in seeing the pictures I brought, especially the ones that included her. She smiled a few times to see so many of her baby pictures taken with me. She was probably thinking that I was not all that strange after all. Who knows, the pictures might have helped to put her at ease with me. I am sure she was wondering if I were her real mommy. What was she thinking about the substitute mommy she had left behind? I know she was a bit confused but she was handling this new situation remarkably well. She was very relaxed which was so amazing to me. I think she was intrigued in discovering I was her brother's mommy. Could it be true that I was her mommy too? I suppose she was not about to jump to that conclusion too soon. I'm convinced that our bonding time gave her some level of comfort in spite of her confusion which she was not able to express. I could only assume she preferred to stick with the familiar knowledge imposed upon her that the German woman was her mother. One could only imagine that all this confusion created by adults was far too complicated for a six-year-old brain to try and decipher.

"Would you like me to take you to meet David?" I turned and asked her.

"Yah, but I go back to Germany tomorrow," was her response.

"Let's meet David, and then we'll talk, okay," I quickly responded. She seemed to have settled for that arrangement for the moment.

She was very excited to receive the things I had brought her, and she was totally diverted playing with them. In the meantime, all the guys were trying to say hi to her.

Mark, who was driving, turned his head around, looked at her in the back seat and said, "You are so beautiful."

She did not respond, only knitted her eye brows a bit and kept looking at her gifts.

A few moments later, Mark inserted one of my music cassettes in the tape deck, and it started to play. We were all clapping and singing, offering our praises unto God for what He had done. I could hardly believe my eyes. Sitting next to me was this long lost little girl of mine clapping her hands, too. She was trying to sing along with us. My heart was overjoyed. She was experiencing no trauma at all. My dream had become a reality before my very eyes. It was as if nothing had happened between us. I kept looking at her and wondering if I really had her with me. It appeared as if it were a dream. Her beautiful face expressed such joy that surprised us. I realized that I had defied the threats of never seeing her again. I had risked my life to rescue her and I was now victorious. I had won the fight. Her rightful place was with me, her mother, who gave her birth. No words can fully express the connection between a mother and the child she bore. It is inexplicable. It is not easily defined. There are no logical explanations for the longing and yearning that takes place when that bond is broken. God designed it that way. She was happy and comfortable sitting beside me instead of screaming for her father. After all, we were a bunch of strangers to her, and there was no logical explanation for her calm behavior. To think, we had just, in effect, re-kidnapped her!

A MODERN DAY MIRACLE

The God of Heaven had intervened miraculously. He had really done it. He had orchestrated all the events so far. He had restored her to me as He had promised in the dream. He had answered my many years of prayers and petitions to Him. He proved Himself faithful to me because my hope and confidence was in Him. I never wavered but believed He was competent and able to do it. He had helped us so far because our faith and hope were in Him. He had kept us safe from danger. He had now healed the years that were lost between us, and He was demonstrating it to me. I could neither cry nor laugh. I was frozen with amazement. All I could do was just to keep staring at her because she looked identical as in the dream that God had shown me. Her hair was the same, her eyes were the same, and even her body size was the same. It was the most awesome moment I was witnessing; God was so accurate. Everything He had shown me concerning Anna was now fulfilled. I was overwhelmed. I was so amazed. I couldn't help but think, "God, you did this for me, you have restored my child to me when no one else could. I thank you so much. I will be eternally grateful to you. I will tell the world what you have done for me. You did what no one else could do. You showed yourself mighty on my behalf."

It finally dawned on me while we were driving that God's ways are not like ours. He works in different ways that we are not able to fully comprehend. When I reflected on the moments that I felt so disappointed that so many organizations were not able to help me, I realized that God had allowed it all. I know now that He knew many things that I didn't know since He is all knowing. He probably spared me many problems had I tried to take Anna when she was in Jamaica. Had the circumstances gone the way I had expected them to, then God would not have received the glory for my recovering Anna. He chose the last organization I contacted to complete the journey because they trusted in Him also. God will not give His glory to anyone else. He wanted me to understand that He would return her to me when the time was right and when all my efforts had failed. He wanted to demonstrate to me that He was still capable of performing a modern-day miracle. He showed me in dreams what He would do concerning Anna before He did it. He assured me in His Word that if I drew near to him, He would draw near to me.

We were now driving on the Autobahn for about two hours when I asked Mark if he could pull into the next gas station so I could use the restroom. Anna decided that she needed to use it also so we both went inside together. It was strange but when we were getting out of the car, I was looking all around me to see if we were being followed, but of course, we weren't. My mind was reliving the fear and paranoia of Paul Silvera.

We returned to the car before the guys were finished filling the car tank with gas. We all got something cool to drink and once more were headed towards Frankfurt. At this point, we were trying to make up for lost time. We missed our exit off the Autobahn since we were all preoccupied with Anna, and as a result, were turned around a few times trying to get back on track. It took us over six hours trying to get back to Frankfurt from Bielefeld. We were all very sleepy and exhausted. Anna was the only one who didn't seem to be affected by this lack of sleep because she had her beauty nap before we got to the apartment.

We finally made it back to the hotel. When we opened the hotel room door, Claudette and her sister were moved to tears of joy to see us with AnnaMaria. I encouraged Anna to go over and say hi to them. She willingly gave them each a kiss and climbed up in Claudette's lap. She showed them her baby doll I had brought her. I was amazed at how friendly she was. It appeared as if she had known them for a long time. She was so much at ease and very comfortable talking with them. Anna's presence gave Claudette much needed hope.

We all collapsed either on the ground or on a bed. The guys slept for a while, but I couldn't. Instead I was making calls to the United States to report the good news. Thanks to the generosity of my friend, Rusty, who gave me a calling card I could use to make those calls.

GOOD NEWS FROM A FOREIGN LAND

First, I called my daughter, Malaika, in Wisconsin and announced the great news to her. She was literally waiting by the telephone as she said when I departed. She was noticeably relieved and filled with excitement; but she quickly cautioned me that Paul would be on our trail. I told her I would call her the minute we landed in Texas. She spoke with Anna and was so overjoyed and told her she could hardly wait to see her. Anna seemed to enjoy chatting with this "big sister" who was actually a total stranger at that moment.

Next, I called my friend, Corine, in North Carolina and told her that I had Anna with me in the hotel. She also said hi to Anna. She was indeed very happy but was now concerned about our safety. She feared that Paul would come looking for us. I then mentioned to her that Mark had suggested that I change our flight arrangements and try to leave with them the following morning so we could all travel together. This was hoping of course, that Claudette would also be able to get her daughter. She was not too happy with that suggestion and told me I should not change the flight but should get out of Germany as soon as we could. After I hung up the phone with Corine, I told Mark that I felt I should keep the original flight arrangements and that I was perfectly comfortable taking a taxi to the airport with Anna. He wasn't too comfortable with the idea, but I assured him that we would be fine. I expressed to him my concern about Paul possibly coming after us. Our flight was early enough in the morning that we would most likely escape an encounter with him. We all agreed that it was the right thing for me to do. We promised to pray for each other.

We carried through our plans even though it was hard for us to be separated. I took a taxi with Anna at around 6:30 a.m. and arrived at the airport around 7:15 a.m. because the traffic was a bit heavy. Mark and the rest of the group, in the meantime, went to the apartment complex where we had seen Claudette's daughter two days earlier in the hopes of her getting back her daughter, also.

The taxi arrived at the airport, and we disembarked, paid our dues, and proceeded inside the main terminal. Needless to say, I was looking in all directions rather discreetly for any signs of Paul. Anna was moving right along with me without any objections. She was somewhat excited to go on the plane to see David.

ON PINS AND NEEDLES

We made it to American Airlines and stood in line to be checked in for our flight to Houston, Texas and then to Miami, Florida. The ticket agent who checked us in at the airport was an American, and somehow, I felt very comfortable with him. It was our turn, and he took our passports and looked at Anna's and asked me how long she was in Germany. I mentioned she was with family for over six months and then my heart started to beat really quickly, and I thought to myself, "This is it! The thing I had feared has now come upon me." I thought for sure he has now caught the discrepancy of no official immigration stamp in her passport indicating when she had entered Germany. I was expecting to be told, "You can't travel out of the country with her, please step aside." I had to do or say something really fast. Those few seconds seemed like hours. Immediately, I realized that I had to divert his attention somehow from focusing on Anna's passport because I could now be detained for questioning. I prayed quietly and asked the Lord to help me and give me wisdom as to how I should proceed. I realized that I had to engage him in some form of conversation.

"What state are you from in the United States?" I quickly asked him since I saw him thinking and trying to figure out what next to do.

"I'm from California." he responded.

"I lived in northern California for five and a half years, and I loved it very much," was my quick response. I then commented on how awful the forest fires were that were currently raging in California and wanted to know if he had family in that area. He volunteered to tell me that his mother lived very close to the area in northern California where the fires were and that he was very concerned about her. I interjected that in a previous fire some friends of mine had to be evacuated and that I hoped his mom would be safe.

"Have a nice flight," he said and handed me our passports without any further questions.

"Thank you," was my response. I was thanking the Lord under my breath and singing my praises quietly.

We made our way downstairs to see if I could find the young man I had met when I arrived in Frankfurt. As we got off the escalator, I could see him at the desk. I walked over to him, and fortunately, there was hardly anyone around. My intention at this point was to share with him what had just transpired in connection with Anna. I couldn't have taken the risk to disclose anything to anyone upon entering Germany in case something leaked out. I felt he was an important link somehow. I just didn't know how.

I mustered up the courage and told him that I would like to speak with him, and so he came from behind his desk. I then revealed to him the reason why I had come to Germany and explained to him that I could not have discussed it with anyone before, for fear of jeopardizing my plans. He understood. I then told him that I was a Christian woman and that I believed the Lord had helped me to get my daughter back. I explained that Anna had been abducted by my former husband over five years ago and that he had relocated with her to Germany. He responded in a very positive way and expressed to me that he too was a Christian. We were now on the same page; I was so happy and relieved.

I then emphasized to him that I felt a bit scared and nervous and wasn't sure if Paul could be in the airport looking for me. He exclaimed how thrilled he was that I got my child back.

He then said to me, "Don't worry. Come with me. I will get you safely to your gate." He told me later that he also worked with security for the airport.

All of a sudden, we were going through all these locked doors that he began opening with his huge stack of keys. We were going through one door after another until finally we got to the upper level of the airport.

"Where are you going with them?" a stern German voice reverberated as we attempted to go through a final checkpoint area. My heart pounded rapidly as I thought we were caught now for sure.

"Here are their passports," my friend said as he took them from me and held them up for the man to see.

We finally proceeded without any further delay. I took a deep sigh of relief as we made it around the corner. "Good heavens," I thought, "that was a close encounter of some kind."

We made it to the gate area where our plane was scheduled to depart. We said our goodbyes, and I thanked him very much. The Lord had provided a human angel to lead us through locked doors and out of sight. What a provision.

I still kept looking all around me to see if I saw that "dreaded face," but we were safe so far. Although I felt safe,

I was not at all comfortable. All I wanted at this point was for the plane to get off the ground and be airborne. If only those people knew how urgently we needed to get out of there. What if he was now in the airport looking for me with the police? What if he told them lies about me? The unknown was too much for me to bear. What if...? What if...?

We walked into one of the stores in our gate area and bought a few souvenirs. Anna was just as comfortable and relaxed as she was when she was with me in the car heading to Frankfurt from Bielefeld. I told her we would be going on the plane soon in order to see David. She seemed happy. She was very anxious to get there to meet him. She asked me a few more times when the plane was going to leave, and I assured her it would be soon.

CHAPTER 10

ON EAGLES' WINGS

"American Airlines flight 71 is now ready for boarding," was finally announced.

It was like I had heard some good news. I was so nervous inside, wondering if someone was going to still show up and escort us from that waiting area before we were able to board the plane. I could hardly wait to be out of there and in the air. Anna was sitting quietly beside me and waiting so patiently too to hear that announcement.

She perked up and smiled at me and said, "Now we go on the plane?"

"Boarding passes please," the attendant said to me.

Those were the magic words I had waited to hear for so long. Minutes at that moment seemed like hours. I was so relieved and happy to present both boarding passes and to be on our way. I took one look behind me, just in case some strange character was headed in my direction to turn us around. "Please hurry people, I need to get on that plane," were the words going around in my head. I just wanted them to close the plane doors so I could be in the air. I wished I could have hurried them along, but I knew I couldn't. I had to contain myself for fear my anxiety would be revealed. I just wanted to close that chapter of my life so badly. If only I could put it behind me. I endured the intense feelings of what could be described as huge knots in my stomach. My chest was tightening, and I had difficulty breathing so I began to take slow deep breaths in order to try and alleviate the undue stress that was upon me. I felt like a zombie and could hardly move. It was as if I was out in the wilds for days, had walked through rugged terrain, and had just returned completely exhausted. If one could purchase sleep, I certainly would without counting the cost. I desperately needed some.

We made it to our seats, and I reached for a piece of chewing gum to offset that uncomfortable, plugged-up feeling I usually get in my ears upon take off. Anna welcomed a piece also. She seemed very relaxed and was also anticipating our departure.

The doors were finally closed, and I breathed that long awaited sigh of relief. Yet, they just didn't seem to be moving fast enough for me. I wanted to feel that plane going down the runway. I just wanted to see that plane take off in case they opened the doors again and called my name in order to have me removed from the flight. I was, needless to say, a pack of nerves.

We made it down the runway eventually and American Airlines flight 71 took off at approximately 10:20 a.m. from Frankfurt, Germany, nonstop to Dallas/Ft. Worth in the United States of America. I then breathed my final sigh of relief, put my head back for a moment, and wondered if it were all real. It seemed like a dream or a figment of my imagination, but when I turned my head and looked beside me the evidence was there, it was real. It was an incredible feeling, even though I was filled with exhaustion. I perhaps had a total of three hours sleep for the entire trip. Yet somehow, my spirit felt as if we were on eagles' wings.

I bowed my head and thanked the God of Heaven for bringing me this far. My prayers of thanksgiving lasted for a few minutes only to be interrupted by Anna telling me she had found a friend who was sitting in front of us. They chatted and exchanged dolls and just had a great time talking with each other. One would think they knew each other from before. Anna told her new friend that she was going to America. She was thrilled when her friend announced that she was also going to the same place. I chuckled at the innocence of their youth and naiveté.

In between Anna's visit with her friend, we got some bonding time. We looked at the pictures I had brought with me once more, and we talked about her being in Jamaica with her Grandma and Grandpa Silvera. She remembered them very well. Of course, she knew nothing about my family except for David, so there was very little that we could discuss on that subject. She told me about her friend Nellie in Germany and about going to France to ride horses.

Both girls figured out a way they could get to sit together because it was more fun. I then decided to put my head back to see if I could try and doze off. Instead, I started reflecting on a dream I had had a few days before I left for Germany. I remembered *being on this plane in the dream, and it took off for Germany from Florida. I got to Germany, picked up AnnaMaria, turned right around, and was headed again for the airport. We then got on the plane and were headed back to Miami.* In the dream, there was no time lost or extra days spent in Germany. Well, I was amazed to see how that dream was also fulfilled. God had shown me once more that He would take me to Germany, that I would get Anna, and that I would just turn around and head back to the United States. That was exactly what happened. We arrived in Germany on Wednesday morning, November 6th, made our way to Bielefeld Thursday evening, November 7th, and picked up Anna that evening then returned to Frankfurt. We flew out of Germany Friday morning, November 8th, 1991 and arrived in Miami that same evening. What was so interesting about all of this was that I took a chance and booked my flight not knowing how all the events would unfold. It so happened that I did not have to change my flight arrangements at all. God was faithful once more to fulfill what He had shown me. I was fully convinced that God had truly helped us. I was also aware of the fact that when He intends to do something, nothing or no one can stop Him.

We finally landed in Dallas; it was an inexplicable moment. It was an exhilarating feeling of freedom to be back within the borders of the United States of America. We were almost home. We gathered our belongings and got off the plane in order to make our connecting flight to Miami. We had plenty of time since our layover would be three hours there.

I immediately found a pay phone and called the office of the American Association for Lost Children in Houston to inform them of our arrival.

"Please make sure you are both wearing your t-shirts with the organization's logo when you arrive in Miami because the press will be waiting there to interview you," we were told by one of the volunteers from the organization.

I was a bit nervous but was ready to share the good news with whole wide world.

I made a few more phone calls to Malaika, Corine, and Lily to announce our arrival in the U.S. I asked Lily to call some other people and inform them too of the news. Malaika was so relieved that we had made it to Texas without any problems. She was extremely anxious to see Anna. She wanted to hop on the next flight to Miami in order to see her. I reassured her that we would get together soon. I promised to call her as soon as we got home.

Anna and I made our way to the restroom and changed into our t-shirts and got all refreshed. She made sure to fix all the cloth hand towels in their clean positions in the restroom while I put some fresh make-up on. She seemed happy, relaxed, and busy. She amazed me at the way she accepted everything. There was no fuss about when she would go back to Germany nor did she ask for her father, step-mother, or half-brother. I was expecting at least a little bit of crying and fussing, but there was none. Instead, there was this amazingly joyous child who was a delight to have around.

After a while, we made it to the gate area in order to wait for our boarding call for Miami.

It was evident from the number of people in the waiting area that the flight was going to be full. We found some seats and made ourselves comfortable because we still had close to an hour's wait. Shortly after we sat down, a group of senior citizens sat across from us. They seemed to have been on a trip together somewhere. One of the ladies noticed the t-shirts we were wearing and inquired about them. I told her they represented an organization that helped me get my daughter back from Germany after being abducted by her father for over five years. Anna was sitting in my lap at that time. This lady was so filled with excitement that she turned around and immediately told all of her friends. Some were a bit choked up, and others were saying things like "God bless you. She is so beautiful. Take good care of her."

A few minutes later, the announcement was given for boarding so we took our seats on the plane and were airborne to Miami. The plane could not get us there fast enough. Anna was showing a few more signs of excitement to get to

Miami to see David. I then starting talking with her in an effort to try and prepare her for meeting the press. I knew all sorts of lights would be flashing as we walked off the ramp. I mentioned to her that there would be some people there who would be very happy to see her and that they might ask her some questions. I told her just to answer them nicely, and everything would be fine. She was extremely agreeable and compliant. She amazed me. What a child! To this point, neither of us experienced any trauma, not even a bit of crying.

HEADLINE NEWS

The plane touched down and taxied to the gate, so we gathered our belongings once more and disembarked. I held Anna's hand, and we began to walk off the plane. As we came close to the end of the ramp, I could hear the rustling movements of cameramen with equipment.

"There they are." I heard someone say all of a sudden.

They could recognize us by our t-shirts. Without any notice, lights were flashing in all directions, and then microphones were hurled in front of us. All we could hear were the clicks of cameras. We were now greeted by ABC, NBC, and other local news reporters, along with a host of friends. We were so amazed at all the attention given to our story. It was truly an amazing moment for us. No words could fully express the excitement that was in the air. Reporters were literally pushing in front of each other to be able to speak with us. It was all now happening. Our feet had touched the ground in Miami, and we were home. We were desperately stretching our necks amidst the crowd of people to see if we could find David. He was no where to be seen with Lily. Where could they be? Could they be waiting for us outside?

"How do you feel at this moment?" Peter Duench from ABC News asked me.

"I thank God for this miracle of getting my child back," I replied as he conducted an interview with both us. "Had it not been for the American Association for Lost Children, I might not have seen Anna until she was an adult," I continued.

"Why did you come here?" he asked Anna.

"I come here to see my mommy and my brother David," she very pointedly replied in her clipped German accent.

We also had another interview with someone from NBC and both reporters followed us all the way to the outside of the airport where Lily was waiting for us with David. He was fast asleep, and she was trying to wake him up to see Anna, but he could hardly open his eyes. The reporters filmed him attempting to wake up. She kept trying to get David to give Anna a kiss, but he was just too groggy. He had no idea what was happening. The moment he had waited for all these years was here, and he was missing it. Poor little guy, sleep was overcoming him. Anna reached over and gave him a kiss on his cheek while he was trying to wake up. Lily gave Anna a teddy bear she had brought for her. She was so surprised and received it graciously.

We finally moved away from the reporters and towards the direction where our friends were patiently waiting. We ended up in the arms of our dear friends, Ernie, Judy, Kelly, and Lauren along with Rusty, Carol, Derek, and Amy who greeted us with welcoming hugs. Donna, who recovered her two boys by the association, was also there to greet us. Donna was a tremendous source of encouragement to me. It was a great reunion. Anna was also given a huge welcome home banner that was filled with messages from many of our friends, some of whom didn't make it to the airport.

We said goodbye to our friends at the airport and drove with Lily and Phil to our apartment. We made it there just in time to hear the 11:00 p.m. news. We were the featured story that night on both ABC and NBC networks. It was quite amazing to see ourselves on the news. Anna and

David were wide-eyed when they saw themselves on the television.

"Wow, Mom, we are really on television," was David's comment.

They were truly amazed. It had really happened. All three of us were at home together for the first time. David and I had prayed so much in that apartment for Anna's return, and now she was there with us. It still didn't seem real. The Lord had truly answered our many prayers. He had restored her to us. Our thanks were unending.

We all got changed into some comfortable clothes. David was very excited to show Anna his toys, especially his little toy computer. Within a few minutes, they were both lying in the hallway in front of David's bedroom playing with it and having a good time. I made a few phone calls while they were *bonding*, to inform some other friends that we were back.

CHAPTER 11

TOGETHER AGAIN

I just couldn't believe my eyes; Anna and David were playing together and having so much fun, no fuss or crying, just sharing. It was obvious they were so excited to be together from all their chuckles. David wanted her to have all his toys. He would give her the shirt on his back if he needed to. He loved her so much. Jesus did answer his prayers, and he now had his sister to play with as he had desired. He was so happy. He was so contented. His joy was full.

We stayed up for a little while longer, but I soon realized that I was running out of steam. If it were up to *those two* they would stay up all night and play. Anyway, without much fuss, we decided to go to bed. That special moment came, and I got to tuck both my children in their beds, pray with them, and kiss them goodnight. I promised myself then that they would never be separated again as long as I lived.

I couldn't help but reflect on the lonely moments I had spent without her before. The many countless nights I had tucked David in and wondered how she was doing. The void her absence created was indescribable. I couldn't help but recapture the hundreds of doubts and fears that had entered my mind at times and had tried their utmost to defeat and discourage me. I realized then that I was on a battlefield for so long, but I won. I was left with the mental scars of exhaustion and stress from that war, but they were worth the fight. I couldn't help but be amazed at the miracle I was looking at curled up in her bed now.

The next morning was Saturday, and my niece Golda could hardly wait to see Anna. She brought her daughters, Johanna and Kristen with her. My two sisters, Kay, along with her daughters, Mariana and Antonita, and Nicky, with her son Robert, also came by. Nicky was visiting from Jamaica. They were also having a great time too with Anna and David. All the new-found younger cousins figured out how to sit on the back of the couch and fall over onto the cushions. Anna then told David to tell me that she was going to stay here "a long, long, long, long time." Needless to say, we were thrilled. She obviously didn't want to part with all that fun.

Mark called me from Frankfurt to tell me that Claudette got her daughter after I left Germany and requested my prayers for them since they were trying to get to Paris and then to Texas. The only problem was that they did not have a passport for the little girl. They ended up at the American embassy in Germany however, and they were eventually given permission to enter the U.S. Another prayer answered. Claudette's daughter's comment to her was: "Mommy, what took you so long to get here?"

THE CELEBRATION

The following morning was Sunday, and it was time for church. Well, when we got there, it was packed. There were close to fifteen hundred people. We sat close to the front section, and we could see Pastor Geoff Buck smiling at us. He had seen the news the night before, and I figured he would call us up to the platform sooner or later to share our good news.

The praise and worship part of the service began and was led by Carl Richardson. As soon as the congregation started to sing the song, "The Battle Belongs to the Lord," I took Anna and David's hands and went forth to dance before the Lord. All of a sudden, I let go of their hands and went forward a bit. I just had a moment to myself where I looked up and realized that God had done this incredible miracle. Tears came to my eyes, and I danced before him in thanksgiving while Anna and David stood behind me. I turned around and realized that they were just standing there, and I went over to them and held their hands once more and began to dance with them. Instantly, people started coming out of their seats and started dancing in the aisles with us. By this time, they had formed a complete procession up and down all the aisles in the church. When I looked at Anna, she was an integral part of it all. She was holding David's hands, and they were dancing together. They were so happy. The Lord had restored our joy, and His spirit was with us. This went on for about an hour. It was the most glorious celebration I had ever witnessed. It was filled with jubilation and praises to God who had answered the prayers of His children. He was worthy of all praise.

After a while, this momentous occasion ended and Pastor Geoff called us to the platform in order to share the incredible rescue story of Anna with the congregation. I spoke briefly for about ten minutes informing them of what had transpired in Germany while Anna and David stood beside me. Everyone was witnessing the miracle first hand.

They had prayed for her and now, here she was, in our midst. At the conclusion, the sanctuary resounded with clapping and shouts of praise.

On Monday morning, we met with a newspaper reporter from the *Sun-Sentinel* newspaper in Ft. Lauderdale at around 2:00 p.m. at the Heritage Park in Plantation. We had our pictures taken along with a brief interview for an article she wrote on Anna's story which was published in the newspapers the following day.

LIE LOW

It was now Tuesday morning, November 12, and I received a call from Mark Miller asking me if I would speak with a reporter from a German radio station who had called his organization in connection with news about Anna. He further explained to me that Paul, my ex-husband, had told them that I didn't have custody of Anna so he wanted me to clarify the issue with the person on the line from the radio station in Germany. I agreed and confirmed that I did have custody of my daughter, so I was asked to fax a copy of my custody to them. I wrote down the fax number and immediately went over to Office Depot and faxed a copy of my custody papers to them. That settled that issue.

I received a few more telephone calls with offers to fly us to different locations in order to do a story about Anna.

Later on that morning, I received another telephone call from one of the detectives in the Cooper City Police Department informing me that Paul had told Interpol that I didn't have custody of Anna. Interpol furthermore wanted me to be turned over to the State of Germany for questioning. The detective told me to lie low until he had handled the problem. He explained to me that he would fax a copy of my custody to Interpol and that I should cut all connections with the press until the issues were resolved. He also suggested that I change my telephone number to avoid being bombarded by the press. I took his advice and immediately changed my telephone number that morning. That ended any contact for us with the press for the years to come, except for one interview I agreed to do with Mark Miller on a program called Something Beautiful, out of Kansas.

Later on that week, on Thursday, I arranged to meet Susan Cohen for lunch. She was the attorney who had helped me with the divorce and gaining custody of Anna. We met at a Denny's restaurant on Miami Beach. This was the first time she had seen Anna or David. She was so delighted to meet them. These were the kids she had worked to help protect. She was a good human being who did her best to help me. I appreciated her so much. Her actions demonstrated that there is still some good left in human beings. I gave her a copy of the newspaper article and a video copy of the television news report. We said goodbye and promised to keep in touch.

The following Monday, we met with a reporter from the *Hollywood Sun* who wrote a very lengthy article about Anna's story. It was on the front page of the newspaper.

The next day, I received a phone call from Mrs. Cole, the Principal of Parkway Christian School, a preschool where David was in attendance. She had seen the television news report of Anna's return and was delighted to know that she was now with me. I had mentioned to her, before going to Germany that I was going to try and get my child back. Her main concern now was why I had not brought them to school that week. I explained to her that I was taking the week off to be with them and also to try and decide what I was going to do since I could not afford for both of them to be there. I also apologized for not calling her before to inform her of my decision.

She said to me, "Don't worry, the board has already met and decided to give AnnaMaria a scholarship." The Lord answered before I called!

AWAY FROM IT ALL

One evening, my sister, Antonia, who also lived in Ft. Lauderdale, called me to say she had received a voicemail message for me from Paul in Germany indicating he wanted to speak with Anna. I did not return his call so he left another message threatening me and my family and that he would send his "men" in for the children if he didn't get to speak with Anna. It gets worse! His next message indicated that the "blood bath" would begin. He also expressed his disregard for the F.B.I. by the offensive language used to describe them. This was enough to scare anyone into hiding. My younger sister, Nicky, who was visiting from Jamaica and staying with my older sister at the time was terrified upon hearing the contents of the message. She immediately gathered her belongings and said, "I'm out a here," and went to stay with a friend that evening.

Needless to say, a certain amount of fear did enter my subconscious mind, and I began to worry a bit. I started looking outside my apartment for any strange-looking character before I would go to my car. It appeared that Paul had a private detective watching us from remarks he made in correspondences to me. The incredible thing was he couldn't touch us. God had His angels watching over us.

So between threatening phone calls from Paul in Germany and not wanting my personal information revealed through contact with the press, I decided to take the kids to the west coast of Florida for a reprieve.

Lily, my friend, and I got them ready and we took off for Bonita Beach on the west coast of Florida on Tuesday, November 19th. The kids had a ball. We watched the dolphins play in the Gulf, walked on the beach, gathered seashells, and played board games. It was a very refreshing time for us. We just had to break away from it all; it was getting to us. We stayed there for three days and then drove to Captiva and Sanabelle islands on our way back to Ft. Lauderdale. We needed a little vacation, and we got it.

THE HOMECOMING PARTY

The prayer group I was a part of decided to organize a celebration party for Anna at Good News Church on Sunday evening, November 24th. Joanne contacted many friends of ours and told them about it. She did an incredible job of putting this party together.

Lily, my friend, contacted Malaika, my older daughter, at the University of Wisconsin without my knowledge, and paid for her airline ticket to be able to attend the party in order to surprise us. So those two pulled off their scheme without my knowledge, and it worked.

On Friday night, at about 10:30 p.m., there was a knock on the front door, and when I opened it there stood Lily and Malaika grinning from ear to ear. They were proud of the fact that they had surely pulled a fast one on me, and I was really surprised. She was there in time for the party.

Needless to say, Malaika was overwhelmed with joy to see AnnaMaria. When both girls hugged each other, it seemed like it would never end. I told Anna that this was her big sister and there seemed to be an instant connection between them. She followed Malaika around and always wanted to sit in her lap.

Many people came to the party and brought lots of presents for Anna. They also brought an assortment of food dishes which turned out to be a real feast. There was so much food that everyone had plenty to eat. It was another great celebration of God's goodness extended to us through friends and family. There was also a beautiful banner made which read: "Anna, Welcome to the Family of God." On it were numerous messages of encouragement to her. I came across the message from Malaika, which recalled the words from her poem, the words she wanted to say to her all these

years: "Welcome home, my sweet AnnaMaria Rachael."
That has been a treasured keepsake.

When we were finished eating, I shared briefly with
the group all that had transpired in my quest to get Anna
back. I ended on the glorious note of "now she is with us."
There was a round of applause of thanksgiving to the Lord
for what He had done in restoring Anna to me.

It was a delightful evening, and we had a wonderful
time. Anna received so many beautiful clothes and dolls
from friends, she had an instant wardrobe. It was truly a
blessing to see how people responded and encouraged
us. Some of the kids even did a dance for her. At one
point, I was wondering what she was thinking. Her facial
expressions seemed to relate the message of "What was all
this about?"

Before it was all over, we had to get Malaika to the
airport to catch her flight back to Wisconsin. When Anna
realized she was leaving, she clung to her along with David
and didn't want her to go. Malaika told her that she had to
go to school and that she would be back to see her. She was
not very happy with that idea but gave her a hug and said
goodbye anyway.

We visited for a while longer with friends and Anna
became very comfortable with her new found pals. David

played a big part in that. There were over two hundred people present. It was truly a memorable evening.

THEY COULD PASS FOR TWINS

Finally, they went to school together for the first time. David was now five years old, and Anna was six. David was reading and writing and ready for kindergarten but he was in a Pre-K class. His teacher had told me many times that he was ready for kindergarten. The work we did at home paid off. Anna was literate in German and could write a few letters of the alphabet, but David was ahead of her. Mrs. Cole, the principal, decided to put both of them in kindergarten so the transition for Anna would be easier. They were so happy to be together in the same class. Many people wanted to know if they were twins because they looked so much alike, and they were the same height. The fact is they are exactly one year and a day apart. They got along so well together that everyone was amazed. Part of this "twin" phenomenon was that they were truly inseparable.

One evening after we got home from school, both Anna and David were sitting at the dining table doing some writing exercises. They were making a lot of progress with their work and seemed to be doing fine. I was in the kitchen preparing supper and making much headway myself. I could see them both from where I was in the kitchen. All of a sudden, I saw this little head pop up in front of the kitchen counter. It was David. With a rather serious tone in his voice, he said, "Mommy, can I marry Anna?"

I said, "No, darling, you can't marry Anna, she's your sister."

To which he responded, "But I love her."

I hugged him and explained to him that brothers don't marry sisters, but it was okay to love each other. What a cutie pie! He loved his sister so much that he wanted to marry her.

For their kindergarten graduation, Anna sang a song in German entitled, "Under the Sea" from the movie *The Little Mermaid*. It was a special treat, and everyone enjoyed it. She was so brave and did such a wonderful job. She got a great applause. She also taught David the song, and at times, they would both sing it together in German. They were such blessings to me.

A SCARE

I received a telephone call a few days later from my mother in Jamaica, informing me that some police officers had paid her a visit in her home in Montego Bay. The reason for their visit, they explained to her, was because Paul had contacted them and informed them that I had abducted his daughter unlawfully from him in Germany and that my mother could easily be harboring me. My mother told them that I was not there and in turn explained to them what Paul had done and also showed them a picture of both Anna and me. The officers ended up indicating to my mother that she would never hear from them again. They also expressed how annoyed they were with what he had done and also for disrupting their day.

DONATIONS FOR A WORTHY CAUSE

We were given permission again, a few weeks later, by Publix Supermarket to be able to collect donations for the American Association for Lost Children. People were very happy to see Anna as one of the children the association was able to find. Anna and David were so cute in the Association's T-shirts, helping to collect money for the organization that had found Anna. We had a great time handing out flyers with information on many children that were restored to the parents with custody. Lily was also there helping us. We collected close to three hundred dollars.

I received a telephone call about a month later from Mark Miller saying that he would like to use our picture on a vending machine project. That meant he would have to fly into Ft. Lauderdale and have our pictures taken. Well, he did, and today we can be seen on vending machines all over the United States. Once a purchase has been made from these machines, a percentage of the proceeds enable the American Association for Lost Children to find more missing children.

LOOKING OVER MY SHOULDERS

I was advised I should make arrangements for AnnaMaria to see a psychologist. My response was that she was fine, and I wasn't sure why she needed to see one. An explanation was given to me that if Paul tried to present a case against me in court that I was an unfit mother, in an attempt to try and get Anna, I would have these reports from the psychologist proving that she was well adjusted and very happy. It made sense so I arranged for Anna to see a Christian psychologist, who ended up not charging us since I couldn't afford his services.

We visited with this psychologist for about four months, and Anna mentioned that they only played games, and he asked her about her dreams. David also sat in with them. The few times he spoke with me, he told me she was doing extremely well, that she had no bad dreams, and she was doing fine. There was no need to continue at that point. My estimation of all this was that I was the one who perhaps needed psychological counseling, not Anna, because she seemed to have been doing much better than I was.

After all, I was the one looking under my bed thinking Paul could be hiding under there in order to snatch Anna and run off with her, or looking in my closet when I arrived at home from work thinking he was hiding in there, too. I just wasn't going to take any chances. I was going to check all the bases just as a precaution; I had valuable treasure on board, and Paul's threats were not to be taken lightly.

We were going on with our lives in spite of the many threats we were receiving from Paul. I eventually gave in and allowed him to speak with Anna on a couple of occasions. I decided after a while that it was not convenient for me to place these phone calls to Germany since there was no financial help from him or his family. Besides, I was not about to give him my phone number to be constantly bombarded with calls from him, so I stopped calling.

Mark Miller called me early in January of 1992 informing me that he was invited to be a guest on a television program called *Something Beautiful* out of Kansas. He wanted both Anna and me to be with him on the show. He was going to be sharing with them about Anna and the miracle of her story. Besides, it was the organization's first successful international case. We were excited to tell what the Lord had done.

I arranged for David to stay with our friends, Rusty and Carol. David would have his friends Derek and Amy to play with. That afternoon, Anna and I flew to Houston, met Mark, and we all flew together to Kansas.

It was a great show. All three of us were interviewed on the program which lasted for about an hour. Anna was a bit shy and did not want to talk much so we did not pressure her. Mark, however, went into detail about the events leading up to and including the rescue. This interview helped to generate some unexpected financial support for the American Association for Lost Children. Many, many people were touched as a result of the television program.

It was great to see Mark again. He and Anna had a wonderful time together, and he now became "Uncle Mark." We all had lunch together after the show and spent some time catching up. Later on that afternoon, we traveled together to the airport, said our goodbyes, and boarded our flights to our different destinations.

One evening after we got home, I received a certified packet from Germany. It was from none other than Paul Silvera himself. He was informing me in a letter that he was going through a legal process that would involve custody of Anna. I simply put it aside and had no intentions of even wasting my time to read it in its entirety. I did notice however that some mention was made of the fact that a private investigator was watching our movements. This confirmed what I found out earlier. I also found out that he had contacted an attorney in the U.S. to try and have my custody order reversed by the courts. The attorney he approached refused to become involved with him based on the established court records. It really doesn't pay to be unprincipled.

A BLESSING IN DISGUISE

A few weeks later, I received a telephone call from the owner of the apartment where we were living. He explained to me that it was the hardest thing for him to do because he was very happy with me as a tenant. However, he had to give me notice to leave since he needed it for his daughter who was getting married. I felt stressed and didn't know what I was going to do. I had been residing there for five years and enjoyed living in that community very much. Anyway, I decided to contact an agent to see if there was anything available for rent in the same community. To my surprise, there was a two-bedroom available, and I rented it immediately. I called the owner of the apartment I was renting and told him that I found a place, and that I was prepared to move as soon as I could make the necessary arrangements. He was relieved.

We left Lagoon Place and moved into Live Oaks apartments in Pine Island Ridge in February of 1993. A few days after we had moved out, I thought I should go back and tell my next door neighbor that we were no longer living there. Interestingly enough, she mentioned that a man with the description of Paul's features knocked on her door earlier that day, asking her if she knew where we had relocated. Since she did not know where we were, she could not give him any information. I doubt she would disclose our location even if she knew, since she was aware of my situation. What a blessing in disguise, the Lord allowed the circumstances to be so arranged that we missed an encounter with the visitor. I am convinced he had come for Anna. He was one day too late, and God was one step ahead of him. May the name of the Lord be praised!

Life continued to be a bit tense and stressed at times. We did not go about it as freely as we would have liked. I was always looking around me with some suspicion as to whether Paul was lurking somewhere watching us in order to snatch the kids as he had threatened. I was constantly watching my rearview mirror, wondering if any strange cars were following me. It was hard to keep a positive attitude and be happy. I battled with depression most of the time. It felt as though no one could ever relate to the lonely moments and hardships I endured. I am sure it would have been possible for me to have done something detrimental in the care and development of my children had it not been for the knowledge of Christ and the hope I found in the Scriptures. I so often thought of my kids and how well-behaved they were and deserving of the very best life had to offer, yet, I did not have the finances by which to make some of it possible. I had to forfeit music lessons at times. We had to buy food many times on a credit card, hoping to pay it back at some later date. Yet, God continued to perform miracle after miracle for us, financially. I am still so grateful for how we were sustained. I realized that I had to live for my children. They were very grateful and appreciative of little things that I did for them. For instance, when they each received a beanie baby for an "A" grade, they were so excited. I realized then that I had to pull myself up many times when I felt the symptoms of stress tormenting me. The tightness in my chest was unbearable, and the severe headaches continued. There seemed to be no relief in sight, but I kept going.

It was an absolute joy to be around my children. The comments were always made to me by teachers and friends of how delightful they were. When I would hear these statements, I would often reflect on the verse in Proverbs which mentions that a good name is to be desired more than riches. I would also note how well they got along together even at home. There were no fights between them. Once I told David, "You should never hit your sister." He had never done that before, but I just thought I would warn him in case he ever had the thought to do it. I also added that Jesus would not be happy if he behaved that way. He was listening very attentively. To this day, he has never hit his sister or been unkind to her. What an honorable guy. Some day, he will make a lady very happy because he took the counsel of his mother, and he loved his sister. With such things, surely the Lord is pleased.

THE BOOGIE MAN

We were enjoying living at Live Oaks apartment since our back yard was a beautifully tucked away park for the community. I still wasn't comfortable with leaving the kids to play alone. I was always being very careful and would sit there with them while they played.

It was now close to the end of October, almost a year after the return of AnnaMaria. My friend Lily had been picking Anna and David up from school and would usually take them back to the apartment in the afternoon. Lily knew how tough it was for me to work and still be there for my two children. She wanted to help in whatever way she could, and this way they could be at home, have a snack, and enjoy some play time.

One late afternoon, at around 3:45 p.m., I received a frantic call from Lily. She had just taken the kids to the apartment and had an encounter with Paul that left her frightened and upset. She informed me that Paul had just left the apartment claiming he had come to see his children. She described him having a coat draped over one arm which looked suspicious to her.

She related to me that as she opened the door and walked into the apartment, the kids followed behind her. She then heard this male voice say, "Don't close the door." She thought it was the plumber, who she was expecting to come at that time, to fix a toilet tank leak, so she continued walking inside, and he followed behind her. When she turned around and saw that it was Paul, she was shocked and scared.

He then said to her, "I'm Paul Silvera, and I'm here to see my children."

Lily said to him, "If you don't get out, I'm going to call the police."

By that time Anna and David had returned from putting their school bags down in their room and were now standing in the hallway looking at him. Anna later told me that he motioned to her to come to him, but she didn't go. Lily also told me later that at that point she was immediately thinking that she was going to be forced to use her karate skills her father had taught her in the event he tried to take the kids. Lily's father, by the way, was from mainland China, and he taught all his kids karate.

When he heard Lily mentioned the police, he turned around and made for the door. At that point, David was crying and was scared so he shouted, "Auntie Lily, call 911."

When Paul left the apartment, Lily secured the door and called me immediately.

A CLOSE CALL

While she was speaking with me, I immediately felt my heart, as it were, go into some sort of a spasm. I could hardly breathe. I took a few deep breaths because I thought

I was having a heart attack. It was so awful. I felt pain and tightness so severe that I couldn't explain it. I kept trying to breathe deeply even though I couldn't get a deep breath. All of a sudden, I felt my heart began to pound. I could hear the thumping of my heartbeat. It was a bit scary. I know now how people can easily have instant heart attacks and die from stress. It was just the mercy of God that I didn't. It was horrible. I still kept trying to deep breathe, and I found myself in so much shock that I could hardly respond to Lily. I told her I would call her back.

After I hung up the phone, I realized that I didn't even tell Lily to call the police and report the incident. I picked up the phone again about ten minutes later and told her to call the police. I was so stressed I could hardly think clearly.

By the time I got home, the police were already there taking a statement from Lily. An officer also took a statement from me and then informed us that we would have to go to the station in order to file a formal complaint.

We both gave statements and filed the report that same evening. That report was instrumental later in my being able to obtain a restraining order to prevent Paul from making surprise visits to my apartment.

This incident took place on October 29th, 1993. Paul called my office on November 4th to inform me that he could have taken the kids if he wanted to when he came to my apartment. He emphasized that he was only demonstrating to me how easy it would be to take them. I told him that due to the new laws passed under the Hague Convention he would be in trouble. His response to me was that U.S. law didn't work in Jamaica and that once he got back there with the children, the laws could not affect him.

I then said to him, "If you won't stop coming around where I live, I will call the police and have you arrested."

His response was, "If trying to see my kids means going to jail, well then, I will just have to go to jail, but it won't be nice after I get there. All I have to do is make one phone call from jail."

He continued to emphasize his disregard for the law. He was such a tormentor. At that point, I refused to speak with him any longer, and so I ended the conversation by simply hanging up the phone so that he would not upset me anymore.

I realized from this recent incident that I needed to get a restraining order to prevent him from coming around us at his leisure without our permission. After all, I could not trust him anymore. He had demonstrated to me that he was not honorable. I could no longer take him at his word. From that dark moment when he lied about taking my 10 month-old to the beach, the trust had permanently been eroded. To date, he had paid no child support and had no intentions of initiating any assistance. He persisted on making arrangements to see the children on his terms and at his own convenience. His actions proved that he had no desires to work anything out in a reasonable way. He continued with this pattern of intimidation and threats, giving me no incentive to collaborate with him. It seemed as if the struggle was starting all over again. I was still so uneasy about what had transpired recently. I was now faced with the nightmare of knowing that our location was no longer a secret. He had found us. The only thing I could do now was to try and protect us as much as possible.

I eventually went before a judge and obtained a restraining order which was sent by certified mail to Paul in Jamaica. He signed for it, and the judge accepted the return card with his signature on it, rendering the order official.

This gave me the opportunity to place Paul on a "look-out" list at the airport, just in case he came into the country again in an attempt to take the children. He was so determined to take things in his hands. He could not wait for the arrangements I was trying to work out with the authorities that would afford him a supervised visit to see his children. He called the Cooper City Police office a few times, wanting to know when they were going to arrange a meeting for him to see his kids. Frankly speaking, no one was in a hurry to accommodate him. The arrangements would have been worked out but because of his behavior and the incident that occurred at my apartment, scaring the kids, I was in no hurry to accommodate him.

NIGHTMARES

I had many sleepless nights and days filled with exhaustion. At times, I would dream that *Paul was chasing me in a building, trying to hurt me, and I was trying to get away.* In one dream, *he finally caught up with me, held my thumb and was squeezing it so hard that I thought my blood supply was being restricted. When I looked at him, his eyes were glossy and evil-looking. I eventually got away.*

Another time, I dreamt that *I was walking with Paul outside a building while we were talking, and something strange happened; I stepped on a rope in front of a metal rolled-up shutter door. All of a sudden from inside the building the ropes were being pulled by some men, and my feet were caught in a trap. The expression on his face revealed that he knew about it, and he looked at the men as if to say, "Aha, we caught her."*

Given my dreams and the way I felt in general about our situation, I had to do everything in my power to protect my children because I was beginning to feel sacred again. The children were so innocent and helpless. I remember so well thinking of ways to try and help them protect themselves in case they were snatched by their father. At this point, Anna was only seven and a half years old, and David was only six and a half. They could be prime targets.

I would think of making associations of places and names for them to remember and be able to tell the authorities in case anything happened. I thought of my brother who lived in Kalamazoo, Michigan and realized that the town he lived in ended with the word "zoo." Besides, I thought most children would remember that word much easier than a telephone number if they were in a crisis situation. So I would say to them, "If anything ever happened, and you were snatched and taken away from me, try to scream as hard as you can for people to hear, then they would know immediately that something was wrong."

I frequently quizzed them by asking, "Where does Uncle Nick live?"

"Kalamazoo," they chimed each time.

I then explained to them that he was the only Dr. Nicholas living in Kalamazoo and that the police would be able to find him easily. Uncle Nick would always know how to find me, I assured them. This drill was done regularly to ensure a back-up plan in case they forgot their home telephone number they had memorized.

We were still living in fear. The children could not play outside without my sitting and watching them. I just could not take the chance of leaving them by themselves to play. Too much had happened; it was a huge risk to take. At least if any attempt was made on Paul's part to try and take them, I would be right there to put up a fight.

We constantly prayed for God's protection. We would not go out of our apartment in the mornings before we prayed and asked the Lord to send His angels to watch over us. When we returned in the evening, we would give thanks that He brought us home safely. Then we would pray at night once more that He would watch over us. God was faithful, and He did hear our petitions, and He did watch over us, confusing all our enemies. If there were unforeseen eyes lurking, watching us, they could not touch us. I firmly believe that there was an invisible demarcation line drawn between us and the enemy. They could not come near us. I would reflect many times on Psalm 34:7: "The angel of the Lord encamps around those who fear Him and rescues them." I know there were angels watching over us.

CHAPTER 12

BEHIND BARS

On Monday, June 20th, 1994, I received a telephone call from the Cooper City Police department. I was informed that Paul was arrested in Atlanta, Georgia on Friday June 17th and would be transported to Florida to stand trial. I was also told that he was charged with the following: burglary, interference with custody, and aggravated stalking.

Then came the terrifying news of AnnaMaria's passport, David's birth certificate, information from a spy shop in Ft. Lauderdale, my license tag number, and address, along with roughly five thousand dollars cash found on his person!

Life now took a sudden turn. I promptly cancelled a trip to Jamaica I was planning to take, the moment I received that telephone call regarding Paul's arrest.

A week later, I received a call from the attorney in Miami, who had helped me obtain custody of Anna. She informed that she had received a letter from Paul's attorney requesting that I drop the charges that were filed against him and try instead to reach an agreement. Needless to say, I ignored such pleas. The table was now turned, as far as I was concerned. Paul was about to reap the seeds he had sown.

I was advised to make sure that the restraining order was updated and enforced. So I had the existing order renewed and served to Paul while he was in jail by a sheriff. I was not about to take any more chances. Besides, he was now on my turf, and this was a perfect opportunity to have the order hand delivered.

Paul had now been in jail for two months. A bond hearing was set for Friday, August 26th at 10:00 a.m. I was not expected to be there but I chose to attend in order to observe the proceedings concerning Paul.

CHOOSING SIDES

To my dismay, the judge made statements in reference to me that were very disturbing. It was made very clear from these statements that he was not in favor of my having gone to Germany to retrieve my child. He mentioned that Paul had not done anything wrong at the time when he took her since custody was not yet established. I was infuriated by some other statements that he made, but I had to remain calm and composed. I was scared that if I said anything or responded with an outburst, the judge might have declared me insane and thrown me out of the courtroom. I was reminded of the verse in Proverbs in reference to fools not having wisdom. I kept reminding myself that I was not going to act like a fool; I would let wisdom take its course.

The state attorney representing me called me to the witness stand. He questioned me concerning Paul's abduction of Anna, in the hopes of convincing those present of the behavior of the man being charged. However, the judge had already set the tone, and it was obvious that there was little consideration for the plight which Paul had bestowed upon me. Paul's attorney tried his best to dissect my character, but his delivery was ineffective.

I began to observe many things, sitting in the courtroom. I noticed Paul's two brothers, sitting in the back of the room. A witness also took the stand on his behalf, and she mentioned that they were living together in Jamaica, and that Paul was a "reputable" businessman. I chuckled quietly to myself. My eyes wandered all over the room, avoiding Paul as best as I could. I studied the design and structure of the room, the judge, his stern expressions, and the sound of the court reporter typing. Then there was another sound. The jingles of the cuffs and chains around the prisoner in the room were inescapable. I finally looked at his feet, then his hands. I saw that he was handcuffed to the chair, and that when he stood up, his pants were slipping a bit due to the lack of a belt. Belts, of course, are not allowed in jails, as they are easy suicidal instruments. How sad! He had been reduced to nothing more than a criminal in chains. I thought of all the threats he had made to me and now, there he was, unable to even speak unless permitted. The "lion" was now quieted; he no longer had a roar. All his malicious behavior had backfired on him.

I reflected on the numerous times I had warned him in telephone conversations that if he chose not to set things right concerning Anna, he would have to answer to the law. However, it was his choice not to heed my warnings, and I was sure he was regretting it now. At this point, there had been no apparent phone calls from jail, as he had threatened. Humiliation had quieted him, and time, it seemed, had taken care of all his threats. On the other hand, perhaps he had come to fear the same law for which he had touted such disregard. It proved to have been far more threatening, intimidating, and powerful than he was. I was also reminded that the Lord had promised to make our enemies our footstool.

That court session finally concluded, and the date was set for a trial before a jury, given the nature of the charges against Paul.

BOND DECLARED YET STILL IN BONDS

The judge concluded that he did not approve of either of our actions with regards to Anna, but he agreed to Paul's attorney's request for bond, which was set at $5,000. This was under the condition that Paul had no contact with the children. A court hearing for the burglary charge was now to be determined. However, in spite of the fact that the bond hearing took place, Paul remained in jail under an INS "exclusion" clause, which gives the INS District Director the right to detain foreign nationals charged with committing a crime in the United States.

During this period of time, I received messages from different sources, including my mother, informing me that Paul's mother wanted to speak with me. His mother did mention to my mother that she was hoping I would consider dropping the charges against her son and trying to work something out. I did not return her phone calls because I did not want to be engaged in any conversation that would entail letting Paul off the hook. I believed firmly that he needed to take full responsibility for his actions, instead of my enabling him to continue with his pattern of repeated irresponsibility.

Some real concerns arose among the state attorneys who were involved in this case as a result of the judge's statements at the bond hearing. In addition, my former attorney was also outraged by this judge's statements. She insisted that I request a change of the presiding judge. I was too confused to think straight. Was this judge just having a bad day? Surely, he would appear less biased by the time the trial began and all the facts were presented. Despite all the efforts being made to try and make the change of the presiding judge, I was partially to be blamed for not aggressively pursuing that change.

My former attorney addressed some issues with the state attorney concerning how things were handled at the bond hearing. In particular, she raised the issue of the judge's statements concerning me which were not very favorable. This caused some commotion, and the attorney representing me stepped down from the case and was replaced by another state attorney. This was most disconcerting for me since this new attorney was not familiar with the case. My former attorney was only looking out for my best interest; my legal ammunition was now weakened.

This new state attorney decided to have my children, along with Lily, my friend, give depositions in connection with the day Paul had entered our apartment in October of 1993. This was crucial because Paul denied that he did. The charges he now faced were directly connected to this incident. He claimed he stood outside the apartment and never entered it. It was now his statement against three witnesses—AnnaMaria, David, and Lily, who all saw him in the hallway of our apartment. The question now was: whose report would the jury believe? Would Paul lie against his own children to save himself? The trial would soon tell.

THE TRIAL

The day finally arrived, and I entered the courtroom in Ft. Lauderdale, Florida on November 8th, 1994 to be questioned once more by Paul's attorney in the trial by jury of Nicholas vs. Silvera. It was a very strange day, and one that was filled with much apprehension and uncertainty. This one was about to be recorded in history. The atmosphere was rather tense, and one could feel the tension in the air. There were no friendly conversations; everyone was quiet and reserved. There was such a hush in the courtroom one could almost hear a pin drop. It was a setting devoid of a pleasant feeling and an uncomfortable one, too. It was a cold, stony atmosphere with a dreary feeling. Human emotions were frozen, it seemed.

Most people had now taken their seats in the courtroom. There were six members on this jury, five men and one woman. This selection of jurors could not have been more skewed and poorly represented. I thought to myself, "What if those men have the mindset of the judge?" Regardless of the outcome, I knew it was in God's hands now. Before I left my house, I prayed and asked the Lord to preside over everything that went on that day. Whatever happened, I wasn't going to worry. I convinced myself that I would not let any unprincipled mortal break me. Paul's attorney tried, but succeed he did not.

The trial started with Paul being questioned by his attorney and cross-examined by the state attorney. His attorney tried pathetically to describe him as a desperate father attempting to see his children. All his questions for Paul were geared in such a way that the jury would have sympathy for him. His attorney also tried to make Paul look good in the eyes of those present by painting a picture of him as being a well-respected businessman in Jamaica. That, of course, was questionable. He also attempted to portray Paul as one who would never do anything to hurt his children.

When Paul was cross-examined, he denied ever entering our apartment. He claimed he only wanted to see his children and also denied ever threatening me.

Next, I took the stand and was questioned first by the state attorney representing me and then by Paul's attorney. Some of the tape recorded messages I had received from Paul in Germany were played by the state attorney who questioned me. They were filled with several threats towards me and my family if I did not return Anna. He also made many disrespectful comments about the FBI and indicated his disregard for them. His language was foul and disgusting. This was heard by all in the courtroom. The jury had enough evidence by this of his repeated threats to us and his constant annoyance. The question now remained, how would they find the defendant in this case?

LAMBS TO THE SLAUGHTER

Needless to say, I was not impressed with the attorney who represented my ex-husband. His attempts at trying to defend him only proved his inadequacies and shortcomings first, as a human being and second, as an attorney. He was totally offensive in his approach. His behavior in the courtroom was distasteful and disgusting. He demonstrated how degenerate one human being can get in order to justify someone else's position. In this case, he was trying desperately to defend his client's wrongdoing. He went to vicious extremes to destroy my character.

First of all, he tried to implicate me as having an affair with one of the detectives. This was an attempt to play a character assassination card which accusation I promptly denied. He tried nearly everything he could in order to make his case seem credible. After all, it was his client behind bars, and he had to get him out, even if it meant defaming someone else's character. Situational ethics, I suppose, afforded him that approach. My response to him was that I did not agree with adultery and that I had the utmost respect for one's marriage.

Next, it was so obvious that he tried to implicate my friend Lily and me as lesbians, since she picked my children up from school most afternoons. He thought that to be unusual behavior for just a friendship between two women. He also wanted to know if Lily had ever spent the night at our house. I told him "No, she had not." The interesting thing was that the children, and I had spent the night at Lily and Phil's house on a few occasions, but Lily had not done so at our house up to that time. His warped sense of "normal" was evident to all present.

That night I had a dream that *I was sitting in one of the courtrooms with Lily, my friend, and two of the detectives who had worked on the case. All of a sudden, I saw a huge pointed metal dart coming out of the ocean towards us through a circular concrete structure. The dart came to the edge of the structure and stopped instead, short of hitting us. Then suddenly it reversed its motion and receded with a suctioning noise into the bottom of the ocean, and I didn't see it again.* I thought of the dream and pondered as to its meaning. The only conclusion I came to was that darts would come against us in the courtroom, but that they would not prevail against us, and that God would put an end to this whole matter. He sure did.

A MONSTER IN DISGUISE

The next morning, I was questioned again by Paul's attorney, and he continued to intimidate me to the point that I had to tell him that he had the right to question me but that he did not have the right to try and destroy my character. It escalated so much that the judge had to interrupt and tell him that that was enough and that those questions had nothing to do with the case. He then refrained from hurling his intruding, insulting questions at me. I give the judge credit for coming to my defense. I stepped down from the stand intact, feeling pity in my heart for someone who could function in such a meaningless capacity. How could he sleep at night? How sad! Nevertheless, I was victorious, because he could not break my spirit. I stood up to him. He acted, in my opinion, like a real monster. I refused to give him the privilege of unraveling my confidence. After all, I was not the one on trial.

Lily's turn came in the afternoon, and she did not fare very well. I tried my best to help her understand how ruthless some attorneys can be given what I had just been through. I reminded her about not letting Paul's attorney upset or discourage her. I tried to encourage her to be as determined in her mind as I was; that no one was worth getting her upset. Try as I may, it was easier said than done.

Paul's attorney got to her and broke her to tears. He was merciless. He failed miserably with me, so Lily would bear the brunt of it all. Oh Auntie Lily, I wished I could have been a little mouse underneath your chair to tell you what to say to him. I wished I could have been there to be able to help you as much as you helped us. Life was so unfair that I was not allowed to even sit in the courtroom and listen. Oh I wished I could have been there to be able to pray for you during those difficult moments. No one will ever understand what you went through for us. Yes, I will always appreciate the great sacrifice you made on our behalf. I remember how scared you were, and the risk you took to testify in court in defense of your 'two little munchkins,' as you often referred to them. They were as scared as you were, too, but I had all the confidence that they would make it, and they did. I was always consoled by the fact that God was with us even in those hard places, and yes, we survived. He promised never to leave us nor forsake us, and He sustained us.

Both detectives who worked on the case held their own. Susan, my former attorney, also stood firm and handled with skill the darts that were aimed at her. She understood the legal jargon that was hurled at her; she feared none of his sly angles.

The agent who had conducted Paul's arrest in Atlanta also testified and did an outstanding job. He conducted himself like a gentleman and answered his questions precisely. Thank you for your conscientious work, officer, a job well done!

ANGELS ON TRIAL

The time had come for AnnaMaria to take the stand and testify. I was given permission by the judge to sit in the back of the courtroom and observe. I was told that I could not interfere with the proceedings. In the event I did, I would be asked to leave. I was obedient and adhered to the rules but I wondered how I would behave if something went wrong during the proceedings, and my child began to feel some form of distress. Would they have to haul me out of the courtroom for contempt of court if I reacted without permission? I was prepared for the unknown, but I realized that I could not do anything to jeopardize my privilege to be present. All I could do now was pray quietly and ask the Lord to protect her and guard her emotions.

Her name was called, and she took her seat in full view of the judge and the jury. She was wearing a beautiful dress which enhanced her natural beauty. She stood out like a shining star in the darkness there and all eyes were upon her. When I looked over at Paul, I could see tears rolling down his face. They were flowing rapidly and uncontrollably for a while. In front of him was seated the miracle child he had dreamed of for years. She was now sitting in front of him under strange circumstances. He could not converse with her nor have any contact with her. He could once presume on that, but it was now out of bounds. How sad! The way that had seemed right to him had now proved wrong. His arrogance did not pay off, and he was now hurting emotionally—his tears were the evidence. Oh, if only he had listened, none of this would have happened. I begged and pleaded but to no avail. This was one of the consequences to his actions. It was truly paying off now, and nothing could stop it. I'm sure he was regretting the choices he had made. Somehow, my pity was not too generous because his payment was well deserved.

His little idol was sitting before him, and he could not communicate with her. The law had set boundaries that had to be respected. She was so beautiful and innocent of all that confusion. None of it was her fault. Was he having a moment of regret as far as how he had conducted himself in the past? He could not contain himself, and it showed. Perhaps he was having a moment of remorse, who knows. Perhaps he was contemplating what he had lost. On the other hand, he might have realized that the emotions that compelled him to snatch her had deceived him. It did not pay off after all, and now he was hurting. He was his own enemy and trapped in the very web he had woven.

His attorney began questioning Anna pertaining to her father's visit to our apartment. She acknowledged the fact that she saw him standing in the hallway of the apartment and that he was inside, *not outside*. He asked her a few more questions, and I was hoping he would not upset her because if he did, I would surely interrupt the process, and of course, I would be removed from the courtroom. There were times that I wanted to tell the attorney to quit asking her anymore questions. Fortunately for him, my child was not traumatized.

Next, my little David took his turn at cross-examination, and he appeared confident. I am sure that deep down, his little heart was pounding, and he was nervous. However, he looked like a poised, miniature gentleman. I was so proud of him. He wore a shirt and tie and looked absolutely handsome. I wondered what all went through his mind. What image did he have of his father? Most little fellows at his age develop strong emotional bonds to their dads. What type of bond was he going to develop? What role model would he have to look up to in his dad? Who would he have to rely on to help him with questions that would arise later on when he needed answers? Would he too be scarred emotionally? Time would tell. The road I could envision was going to be very rocky. I could only try to do my best.

This was Paul's first opportunity to get a good look at David. When he had entered the apartment and had to leave in a hurry, he briefly saw David. Now his son was seated in close proximity to him, and neither of them had ever spoken to each other. How odd—father and son, strangers to each other. David was now almost eight years old and did not know his father. He had always said to me that he wanted a daddy like his friends at school. His little heart ached for what was supposed to be. I, on the other hand, felt so sorry for him that he was being shortchanged in life. What would he be thinking now, seeing his father chained to a chair? Or did he notice at all? Did he realize that that was his father sitting there? I would have liked so much to know what was going on inside his wee brain. He was far too young and innocent to be going through this ordeal. If only I could spare him the agony of this saga. If only I could erase these moments for him. Try as I may, I couldn't.

He was asked similar questions to the ones Anna was asked about his father's visit to the apartment. He also acknowledged that he saw him *inside* the apartment. The questions were few so his time there was brief. I was so thankful for that.

I met both my children outside the door of the courtroom where Lily and I were waiting patiently for them. They were escorted by someone from the child advocate service. They did exceptionally well emotionally, and I was happy for that. I abhorred the thought however of having my children put through such an ordeal. They claimed it was necessary in order to confirm testimonies in front of a jury. It was now their word against his. How would the jury respond?

TIME SERVED AS RECOMPENSE

It was now Monday, November 14th, 1994, and the jury finally reached a verdict. Paul was found *not guilty* on all three counts! We were hoping at least that they would bar him from entering the United States. No such luck. The card his attorney played in front of the jury concerning his client's desperate attempts to see his children seemed to have worked. The five men on the jury obviously showed their partiality. The one female on the panel who might have voted her conscience and perhaps voted objectively was obviously overruled. It was noted, however, that if Paul entered the country, I should be notified by the authorities.

So, my ex-husband was able to leave the U.S. a free man without even a misdemeanor charge, given all the substantial evidence that was presented against him. He still paid for his "sins," though, by serving five months in jail. That was recompense to us for all that we were made to endure. Hopefully, he was taught a lesson.

What seemed to be most disturbing was the fact that Anna's, David's, Lily's, and my testimonies held no weight against Paul's testimony in the courtroom. What was even more outrageous was the attempted character assassination of me by Paul's attorney and the implications that Lily and I were lesbians. If that wasn't bad enough, there was the additional implication that I had an affair with one of the detectives handling my case, and the worst implication of all, that I was involved in voodoo.

Never had I been so humiliated or insulted in all my life. The courtroom from my experience appeared to have been reduced to a mere circus where unethical and unprincipled people were given, as it were, a free rein to intimidate and malign other people's characters and were allowed to get away with such acts under the disguise of the legal process.

There was one consolation I had, and it was simply this: my children and I told the truth even though it held no weight in a court of law. The question I ask is: What confidence can we have in such a system? I am afraid, not much! Truth today, unfortunately, has been redefined by such detrimental concepts as "situational ethics." Whatever happened to good, old-fashioned truth, honesty, and integrity, which are the building blocks to any sane society? Paul's attorney might have felt that he won a case for him, but in all reality, he was a loser in terms of ethics.

As hard as this was for me to accept, I knew that God was still in control of it all. Who knows what could have happened if Paul was given a conviction. He might have become angrier, and many awful things could have happened to us by way of revenge. In this way, perhaps the Lord allowed him to feel fortunate to be able to get out of the U.S. without further problems. To my knowledge, he has not returned since then. So it worked out for the best in a number of ways; he thought he won, and we got rid of him. I am positive that he was hesitant to reenter the U.S. for fear of the unknown. The Lord's ways are unfathomable.

EPILOGUE

Thirteen years have now passed since we were reunited with AnnaMaria. She is now nineteen years old, and David has turned eighteen. They are exactly a day and a year apart so we have one birthday celebration traditionally, and they looked forward to it each year. Last year, however, they decided they wanted their birthdays to be celebrated on their separate days. We did, and they were very special. They have often been referred to as the Silvera twins by their friends. They resemble each other very much; however, David now towers over Anna's head and is 6' 3" in height. One of his dreams has been fulfilled—he can now dunk a basketball.

The following year after the trial ended, on July 30th, 1995 we received a telephone call which the answering machine picked up. It was Paul calling from Jamaica, and he left a message saying he would like to speak with his children, but of course, we did not return the call. He called a second time, but we still did not respond.

He called again around Thanksgiving time, and David answered the phone.

"You are a bad daddy; you treated my mommy bad," he said, when he realized his father said hello to him. He then handed me the phone and just collapsed in my arms.

I hugged him and told him it was okay. He had bottled up those feelings in his little mind, and now they had come out with an extemporaneous gush. It was the truth, and he had confronted his father and told him how he felt. He was so nervous, but we assured him that he was a trooper and gave him a lot of encouragement.

It was so sad that a young child like David had to say such a thing to his father. It was, nevertheless, the truth. I am sure Paul had to think about what his son had to say to him for a long time to come. He could have been enjoying him, had he made good choices. He could also have been experiencing his development and helping to guide him along with good fatherly advice. Instead, he forfeited his chances of building a sound relationship with him. All young boys need a father to bond with and learn from. What role model was David going to have now? He was so deserving of a good, loving father. He would have no father figure to get advice or to gain counsel from. He would have no one to take him on hikes or ride bikes with or do the things a father does with a son. What would be his model of marriage? Paul clearly was now reaping what he had sown. Whose fault was it?

On June 22nd, 1996, we received another telephone call from him, but this time I happened to answer the phone. His comment to me was that he knew I was still mad at him. I told him that I wasn't anymore, but instead, I felt pity for him. He asked me if I could find it in my heart to forgive him, and let us move on. I told him yes, that I had forgiven him, but I would like to be left in peace.

His next comment to me was that he wanted to speak with Anna, at which time, I informed him that she did not want to speak with him. (My reason for saying that was because she had told me in advance that if he called again, she did not want to speak with him.)

"Let her tell me that herself," was his response to me.

So, I called out to Anna to pick up the phone, but she wouldn't.

"I don't want to speak with him," she yelled back.

I repeated to her that her father wanted to speak with her, so she picked up the phone.

"Hello," I heard her say since I remained on the line.

"Hello, Anna, this is daddy," he said.

"Paul, why did you lie against me in court," she insisted.

First of all, he was shocked at her referring to him as "Paul," instead of "daddy." She was obviously very mad at him, and it was now coming out.

"No, no, this is ridiculous," her father grumbled.

"You said you did not come inside the apartment, and I saw you in the hallway," she retorted.

"No, sweetheart, I stood outside; I didn't come inside," was his comeback, but to no avail.

"No, you were standing inside," she emphasized.

He was still deceiving himself by believing his lies. I guess he had to keep his statements consistent for fear they could ever pose a problem for him. I don't know!

"Why did you take me away from my mommy and tell me that another woman was my mother?" she continued.

There was a silence, and then I made a comment about it all backfiring on him. He started shouting that I was only brainwashing the children, at which point, I hung up the phone. I was not about to let him upset and intimidate us anymore. I had had enough.

"Mom, I wished you hadn't said anything, because I was going to tell him that he needed Jesus in his heart," she said with all seriousness.

We have not heard from him since that day and to date, it appears as if he has never given thought as to whether his children needed to eat food or wear clothes. That tells a lot about his character, doesn't it? I wonder how he could function knowing that he abandoned his children in more ways than one. He has always had our address, but it was never used for the purpose of sending any financial help for them or finding out how they are doing. All I ever received were his threatening letters and notifications of his new found plans to take Anna from me.

We no longer live our lives in fear. We have somehow survived in spite of the odds that were against us. We saw how God became our Helper and our Protector. He was the one who caused people to give to us generously; I was like a widow, and my children like orphans. However, all our needs were supplied, and we lacked very little. We always had clothes to wear and food was always on our table, and we still had some to share with others. My children never went to bed hungry; our needs were always supplied.

Anna and David continue to be a delight to my soul. They have made good choices and have also formed good friendships. They have a wonderful relationship which involves mutual respect and love for each other; they are true buddies. There have been a few arguments, but there has never been a fight or really harsh words spoken between them. I believe they captured the essence of true Christian living. They both attend church in addition to their college group where they receive a lot of encouragement.

They have also been the recipients of many awards and scholarships at the different schools they have attended. David kept an unbeaten track record from second to fifth grade in the one-hundred-yard dash. Anna was equally fast and also held first places in the girls' races. They were also published poets in *A Celebration of Florida's Young Poets* in 1996.

In the summer of 2001, they both had the privilege of attending the Worldview Academy Leadership Camp at Wake Forest University in North Carolina. They both felt it was one of the most important events they had attended so far that had encouraged and confirmed their Christian worldview.

In November of that year, AnnaMaria was selected to represent Kennesaw in the Junior Miss America pageant that was held in Atlanta, GA. She was placed in the top fifteen out of roughly two hundred and thirty girls. She was excited and thought it was an incredible experience.

Shortly after this event, they were invited to become Student Ambassadors to the United Kingdom, and then in 2002, the same invitation was extended for Australia. They also became members of The National Society of High School Scholars.

They both love music very much and also play different instruments. Anna plays the flute, thanks to my sweet friend Tesse who gave her lessons after she arrived from Germany. She plays at different times in the orchestra at church, and David plays the guitar for the high school and college groups at church. He also played the trumpet in his middle school band. He loves basketball and played on the varsity team for his high school.

He has always wanted to become an Air Force pilot but now his interests have shifted towards business and finance. Anna, on the other hand, was interested in Law, but now her interests have also shifted towards medicine or psychology. It will be very interesting to see what careers they end up choosing.

They both graduated from high school and made it into Who's Who among American High School Students for two consecutive years, 2001-2003. They started their freshman year in college in Georgia in the fall of 2004 and will begin yet another phase of their journey.

Malaika, my oldest daughter has completed her medical degree from Stanford University, completed her Residency Program in Otolaryngology (ENT) and is now a surgeon. She made it after all, and needless to say, I'm extremely proud of her. She has been quite a role model for Anna and David, and they look up to her and love her very much. Anna calls her "Sissie."

She got married in December 2002, to one of her colleagues, Cameron, a general ENT surgeon as well. As far as David is concerned, he has been given the "rite of passage" into our family without reservation since he is also a big Star Wars fan.

Over the years, I have reflected on how grateful and appreciative my children have been for the simple things I did for them. Most kids would take such things for granted, but not mine. They demonstrated their thankfulness in a myriad of ways and quite secretively, too. Gifts and flowers were bought under my nose, so to speak, without my knowledge.

David was the watchman many times in the store or supermarket to make sure I didn't get to the check-out stand before AnnaMaria had a chance to quickly pay for items they had both schemed to purchase and then have well hidden in the car to be retrieved later.

I remember also Anna and David's first trip to Michigan. They left me notes all over the house. Without trying to find them, they would appear on my dresser, my nightstand, in the pantry, and on my bathroom sink. These notes would read, "Mom, I love you and will miss you so much." To this day, they still leave me notes when they go away for short trips.

Mother's Day has always been a treat for me. Once, Malaika was home on that occasion, and she joined in on the plan to surprise me by helping to make breakfast and have it served. Of course, I had to select my choices from a menu that was created by Master David.

I have dried and kept many of the special roses I received from all three of them, especially from the beautiful bouquets I received from Malaika. Her cards to me over the years have truly been encouraging. In one she wrote, "Thanks for being a mom that I can be proud of, and who is still giving her all for her children." In another, she wrote, "I have only one thing to say this Mother's Day: I would never have made it this far without you."

David wrote in one of his cards to me for Mother's Day: "You are the best mommy in the world. Thank you so much for doing all that you do. You have given Anna and me so many great opportunities in life and memories that I will never forget."

Anna's card to me Mother's Day, 2002, is very special because it sums up beautifully how she feels. This is what she wrote:

A mother's love is indescribable
It remains a mystery, yet undeniable
No one can quite match this love,
For it is God's own specialty from above

Love that chases dark clouds away,
Removing sorrow, guilt, or pain
Love that gives, and never expects
Love that loves enough to stay

This love just doesn't wear out
It keeps on loving
Erasing worry, fear, and doubt

A mother's love is priceless
Nothing can compare
It holds many secrets,
Yet loves enough to share
When no one else will help you,
When no one else will care
A mother's love is willing
To listen and just be there

Where would we be without such love?
Could we even survive?
It seems to keep the world in place
The reason why we're alive

Sometimes this love is taken for granted
People tend to misuse it
Others simply demand it
It seems so easy to simply love someone
But we don't realize how precious this love is
A mother holds the future in her hands
Her guidance and input determine her
kids

I know I want to be just like my mom
A person of wisdom, truth, and knowledge
A person whose actions truly reflect
Someone who others admire and respect

I'll never be able to return such love
To make my mom proud is what I desire
I can only accept it and do my best
To set my goals and reach even higher
I hope you know I hold you dear,
And thank you for your effort and time
To success itself, you've brought me quite
near
And helped me make my little light shine

I'll never forget all you've done
The way you taught me to be who I am
To keep on trying, and never give up
I hope you know you've truly won

I count my blessings everyday
And realize how lucky I truly am
For God sent you my way
To teach me right from wrong
To let me know it would be ok,
Even though the road seems long

Mom, you always seem to brighten my day
To call you mom is such an honor
And a delight to be called your daughter
I want you to know how much I love you,
How much your love truly means

One day I'll be able to repay you
But not in the same way you loved me
See mom, your love is irreplaceable,
And no one will ever truly see
The secret, the joy, mystery
To a mother's love

Happy Mother's Day, Mommy.

I love you,

Anna

APPENDIX A

1. Jeremiah 32:27: "Behold, I am the Lord, the God of all flesh; is anything too difficult for Me?"
2. Psalms 34:15: "The eyes of the Lord are toward the righteous, and his ears are open to their cry."
3. Psalms 40:1: "I waited patiently for the Lord; He inclined to me, and heard my cry."
4. Isaiah 41:13: "For I am the Lord your God, who upholds your right hand, who says to you, Do not fear, I will help you.'"
5. Mark 11:24: "Therefore, I say to you, all things for which you pray and ask, believe that you have received them, and they shall be granted to you."

(New American Standard translation)

ABOUT THE AUTHOR

Maria Nicholas is a first-time author who took much pleasure in writing from an early age. Her background in the communication arts led her to participate in the production of a feature film and then later joined the faculty at a local business college as a lecturer in business communication skills. Her teaching experience transported her to the other side of the globe - —the Middle East - —where she experienced war-torn Beirut, Lebanon, for one year. Her travels also took her to Jerusalem, the Acropolis at Mars Hill in Athens, and a discovery of her father's roots in Cyprus. She has served on different boards in her community and currently teaches a ladies' Bible class at her church.

Maria Nicholas, born on the island of Jamaica, is now a U.S. citizen. She graduated from high school in Jamaica and from Western Michigan University in Michigan. She currently resides in Georgia with her daughter, AnnaMaria, and her son, David. She has considered it a privilege in sharing this inspiring story at speaking engagements, and invariably, she has been encouraged to publish this experience for the world to read.

To order a copy of this book contact:
AuthorHouse
Toll Free: (888) 280-7715
www.authorhouse.com
www.thousandsoftears.com

For speaking engagements write to:
Maria Nicholas
P.O. Box 926
Kennesaw, GA 30156
toftears@bellsouth.net

Printed in the United States
42547LVS00001B/38